BAILEY

Other books by the author:

Underwater (1974 and 2014)

Trespass (2013)

Rematch (2021)

Family Money (2022)

BAILEY

a novel

JOAN HAWKINS

Landon Books
NEW YORK

First Published by
Landon Books, New York, 2011
First Edition (electronic) by
Landon Books, New York, 2011
Second Edition (print) by Landon Books, 2012

www.JoanHawkins.net

ISBN 978-0-9837348-2-6

Book and cover design by www.Cyberscribe.eu

Chapter 1

She said that Bailey was her name, her only name. Never had the medical staff at Stockbridge known a patient to dry out so uncomplainingly.

Although at fourteen years old she was the youngest alcoholic ever admitted to the exclusive sanitarium, Bailey looked like a matron with a rough-skinned, red fleshy face and a portly body. From the morning she arrived, she appeared to accept Stockbridge as an unloved child does camp. Often melancholy, but always stoical, she made herself at home as quickly as she could. She remarked at once that the buildings and the grounds reminded her of a country club, which was considered astute, because between the two world wars, Stockbridge had been a luxurious resort for golfers at the edge of the State's western hills.

Bailey loved the food at Stockbridge. She chatted with the waitresses and walked into the kitchen to compliment the cook on the spaghetti. She loved her corner room with two windows on the third floor; and the carpentry shop, where she set about making a model of her childhood home. She walked about with a shy smile and a quick, light step. She greeted the other patients with a slide of her hand, palm out; moving between them as though to erase their general irritation. At this, the hostility of Jim Peabody, the sanitarium's youngest male patient disappeared as though her sliding palm were a magic wand.

"Suck shit, man." Bailey's cheerful tone challenged the twenty-two-year-old's frigid composure. On the spot they became the sanitarium's famous young couple. Snobbish, reclusive, Jim Peabody accepted the girl's foul-mouthed adoration as though it were his fate. That they were drawn together by the symmetry of their delusions became the staff's favorite witticism. The girl thought she'd castrated her father while the boy was convinced that his father had castrated him.

Jim Peabody's pretensions to grandeur angered the Stockbridge medical staff. Ignoring the psychiatrist in his mandatory therapy sessions, he read books on military history. His father had been the youngest captain in the American Army before becoming a famous doctor, and it was his mission at Stockbridge to prepare himself for the day his father died. As the future head of a distinguished family and the custodian of his father's fame, he had no time for the soft knowledge of introspection and memory.

His decade of alcoholism, the cause of his Stockbridge stay, he repudiated with lordly aplomb. Drinking was a hazard of the socially powerful – not a disgrace. Always it had been the cover for impossible crimes that could not be exposed. It was obvious, wasn't it, what the facts on his admission chart must be?

Bailey, however, with her shy courtesy and democratic respect, her graceful heft and fine eyes, was immediately the sympathetic focus of opinion and anecdote. Her devotion to Jim Peabody, and her submission to his schedule of self-improvement, combined with her explosive prurience in his presence, were thought to point to a reality that reversed the current of aggression, making her its victim. The child of alcoholic parents, neglected by her mother, by her father abused, Bailey endured her load of unconscious agony with the same strong grace with which she bore her fat.

If an intern were idealistic and vigorous, Stockbridge Sanatorium was the most depressing residency one could pull. Since the owners had no intention of coping with the acutely disturbed, only the alcoholics and the senile paid the enormous bills.

In this swamp of decadence the friendship of the oddly aged youngsters provided relief to the underused staff, who named their process "The Volcano." Under the pressure of Bailey's pornography, it was at first thought that the terrible weight of their repression would blow sky-high, leaving them supple, hopeful and bound for the world.

Then it was circulated that the meeting of the two strangers was only apparent: the young man's famous father was paying the shocking bill for them both. A sinister contrivance was felt to be at work.

At table, walking in martial unison through the halls, and especially when they stepped out of the thick woods at the edge of the golf course, at the end of their afternoon walk, they looked to be escaping some great fright, as Hansel and Gretel had fled the witch. But the powerful figure that controlled them both could only be killed by the truth and not by the phantoms of a grandiose egotism that only the wealthy and the insane could sustain.

Not one of the idealistic interns leaving Stockbridge at the end of their term kept the young people in mind. It was too depressing.

Bailey lost the last point with a casual lunge of her racket and jogged smiling to the net. "Suck my ten-incher, girl — you pussy player."

Returning the yellow tennis balls to the can, Jim looked at his unique friend with imperturbable eyes.

"Sore loser, kid. I just played your backhand."

"You played shit, sister."

As Jim turned his back to her, Bailey raced around the net and stood at his side, timid and afraid. As always, her nervous contrition induced in Jim the sensations of a person he'd never before felt himself to be. Intellectually brilliant, of compelling moral influence, he apparently inspired in Bailey an almost helpless worship. To costume this person in proper attire, three weeks previously he'd written his mother, asking her to send up his father's riding boots and the short khaki captain's jacket that he'd worn in the previous war. The feeling of the jacket and boots, their image in reflecting surfaces, confirmed the girl's admiration in glorious reality.

"My mouth just opens, Jim. I never know what I'm going to say. I never feel mad at you."

Bailey's keen, constant and uncritical appreciation was the furthest from hostility that Jim could imagine. An eruption of her unfortunate social background was the only way he could explain these profane geysers. No soap in her mouth as a youngster, he supposed; never been whipped as he had, or locked in a room. While it was probably too late to introduce physical punishment as a curb to her hysteria, he was determined to eradicate her vulgar accent.

Flat and blunt, the harsh tone of Bailey's speech would alone encourage mental depravity, but Jim understood the brain. Accommodating different sounds, Bailey's brain would develop different pathways. The old ones, tormented to near epilepsy by ugliness, would dissolve, and with them the filth of her helpless tongue.

"I never see any anger, Bailey," Jim smiled at her. "I never feel any, but what I hear has got to stop. It will be stopped! We're working on the problem. In fact," he glanced at his watch, "we have an hour and a half before dinner. I'll shower, dress and bring the tape recorder to your room in twenty minutes. What's this? Do I see mutiny in your eyes?"

Jim laughed at his extravagance – could a kitten be a lion? Then pushed Bailey forward. Accustomed to the girl's alacrity, he stopped at her grudging weight. Bailey looked down at her sneakers.

"It makes me sick talking different."

"Talking correctly."

"Talking like mother, talking like you – it makes me sick."

"I know it's a strain at the moment. But you know our way, Bailey. An hour a day and very soon no one at Stockbridge will believe you ever sounded like a guttersnipe."

"Fuck you!" Bailey shouted and for the first time her straight-on eyes were grim.

"I beg your pardon."

"I like doing math and reading and learning about history, but it makes me feel awful." Bailey peered up at the sky as though to drain the ache in her throat. It made her miserable that Jim hated the way she'd spoken since birth. She pitied her father, whose accent had offended squadrons of aristocratic ears.

"How do you think I feel when you talk filth? Do you think I can live with that indefinitely? Do you think you're tolerable if you're not working to rectify the situation?"

"Fuck me! It's not my accent that swears."

"Your mindless obscenity is a habit, Bailey. When you learn to speak the King's English, you'll be relieved as well as me."

"My ass!"

"Your future." Jim marked his humor with a stiff smile. "I want you out of the shower, dressed for dinner and seated at your desk in twenty minutes. You will learn to speak like a lady, Bailey." Walking off, Jim waved his hand over his shoulder, "twenty minutes."

"Don't leave me! Help me!"

Chapter 2

Out of Jim's presence Bailey was frightened at Stockbridge, especially in the halls and dining room of the sanitarium where the patients looked like dead fish as she passed their erasing eyes.

Back home Bailey had had her vodka to dull the pain of her family's dislike – and a day-long slide of television shows to pass the time. But at Stockbridge the same programs pushed her out of her corner room to the winter woods where she first saw Jim Peabody, a wintry tree himself with his numb, serious tolerance.

"Your father sucks shit," she'd been quick to inform him.

Looking up from his fly, Jim observed the blush of her ferocious shame with bleak, quiet eyes. "Worse than that."

Jim acknowledged her anxiety and terrible tongue with total indifference to their cause.

"All the Stockbridge patients are dead fish," he allowed with a frosty smile. But he and Bailey would not drown in the past, as other patients had, but work every minute of every day to survive in the future.

As Jim's schedule and sarcastic patience blocked off the past – she'd learned tons in a year – Bailey was just as happy as she'd been at home when locked in her bedroom and enthralled by the truth and beauty of the television dramas. But this year she wasn't drinking. Fear stepped back while Jim worked with her. She was horribly obscene. Out of nowhere, waves of filth smashed against Jim's rocky composure. Oh, the deep lines in this boy's face, as though age had made a mistake and drawn itself too soon. His patience and glancing humor, like ice shining in the sun, had saved her from a fear that had kept her on her feet in aimless wandering, that had made her eat too much and turned sleep into the goal of her days.

Jim was a god with his feet in her life. Like a dog, she'd allow herself to be trained, but she was deeply ashamed when she heard her "acceptable" voice on the tape recorder. A dog putting on the dog.

Brick building turning black. "Twenty minutes," Jim commanded, still in sight as he walked through the evening shadows. There were snakes in the ivy patch and doves cooing as if to give voice to the loneliness that Bailey could no longer endure. Groaning, she plunged in a tip-toe rush towards a lesser dread.

Chapter 3

An hour before supper Jim Peabody knocked on Bailey's door. Admiring the fresh shine of his riding boots, he relished the emphatic clicks of his heels as he trod the linoleum halls to Bailey's room. His boots, captain's jacket and powerful tape recorder were his silent insistence that the reform of her speech must continue.

Bailey lifted the model house from her work table to make way for the tape recorder. "Hold it, Captain, the glider plane fell down." She put glue on the end of a thread and stuck her hand through the open back of the well-made house. Crouching, she looked through a window.

"Fuck me! It's turning on its string." She lifted her thrilled eyes to Jim. "It's got a shadow."

Jim looked at his watch, his boots creaking with impatience.

Putting the model house on her dresser, Bailey came back to the table. "I like the way I sound. I talk like my father."

"We'll both survive our fathers, Bailey – with work."

"You sure survived my sister, Cary."

Setting up the tape recorder, Jim did not hear Bailey's flash of bitter resentment. When he pulled the chair from under the desk and sat, Bailey had taken her favorite perch on the end of her bed. Accustomed to the folded legs and straight spine of painful effort, Jim disliked the sag of her shoulders and head as she leaned back against the wall, her legs stretched slackly in front of her.

At the soft hush of the turning tape, Bailey glared at the severe young man so proudly wearing his powerful father's war jacket and dismally listened to her mother's elegant accent erupting from her chest.

"Captain Peabody! You must educate yourself. You think Cary Bailey is meat in the supermarket, the chicken and the steak, don't you know. All wrapped up tight in that glossy stuff. You made a hole in her wrapper. Her juices made a mess."

"You've got it, pal." Jim's eyes brightened in icy pleasure.

"Cary adores housework, can you believe that? In bed, watching the cartoons I'm astonished by her drudgery. The speed of achievement is essentially the appeal of cartoons. Real life demands such laborious effort."

Bailey's revolted eyes dropped to Jim's trousers. "In a cartoon I'd be fucked blind in an instant, but you – clip clop, clip clop, over hill, over dale – such a bore."

"All our work is to such good purpose, Bailey. I'd almost swear to our common heritage. By God, I'm proud of you."

Bailey sickened in the stream of his pride. Panting, her arms and legs spread wide on the bed as though her weight had become a crushing stone. Her face and neck were red and wet. "I'm too full to go to supper. Full of SHIT!" Bailey shouted in her native speech.

Jim bristled at her ugly voice. "You're full of your past," he sneered.

"The unspeakable past, the past of the entire human race – so what? The unconscious lust of fish and bugs and reeking mammals is violent poison in our guts. Be glad of the eruption. You'll be clean all the sooner for the violence – but don't brood."

"It's your past too." Regarding him in sallow despair, Bailey seemed to threaten the grip of her clothes with her pasty expansion. Jim could almost see her buttons flying. "Whenever you make me sound like a broken jaw, Jim, your past comes out of my mouth."

"I don't pay attention to your fantasies, kiddo. Shall I explain to you again the impossibility of any social connection between our families?"

Bailey crawled to the top of her bed and curled round her pillow. "You don't like me."

"No! No! No! Not the old voice," Jim clapped his hands like an irate schoolmaster. "Your old voice is gone forever. I never want to hear it again."

Bailey got to her knees to pull the yellow curtain across the window then crashed down around her pillow.

"Get up, damn you!" Jim snapped back the curtain, and opened the door.

Answered by the girl's woeful silence, Jim slammed her bedroom door. His clicking heels sounded hollow in his ears as he went into the large dining room to eat his supper alone.

Chapter 4

In front of the clubhouse Bailey swung up on the stone lion that guarded the granite steps. Its twin lay vigilant a few yards away. In the long, imaginary rides she used to take with her brother Tom, that was always his mount. Now, he'd "matured" as he mockingly called it and played golf as often as he could manage. Bailey spotted him this very minute, hopefully beyond the range of the ball that Peabody was about to smack off the first tee. The long, green fairway probed the distance, narrow as a tree trunk, when Bailey lost the view. The red flag at the second hole caused the child to straighten her back as she rode and clenched the stone lion with severe pride.

It was after supper, five days before her tenth birthday, and the serious excitement could begin. Like a stoker at a fire, Bailey watched over it. She fueled it gently, the bellows of anticipation barely used, then, on the last night, extravagantly pumped.

Mrs. Peabody teed off and waved to Bailey on her perch. Bailey admired the sharp creases of Dr. Peabody's trousers, their intense whiteness. Tennis players had to wear white while the golfers were allowed to wear what they liked. Bailey wouldn't dream of being a golfer. Wearing whites was a rule she vehemently approved of. Men had to wear jackets and ties in the dining room and no woman in slacks could eat anywhere in the club. Her father would not lower the standards for anyone. Not even the President of the United States could sit in the bar or dining room in his shirt sleeves, although he might be allowed to drink his cocktail on the terrace.

It was the oldest country club in the entire nation and, Bailey had no doubt, the richest and most beautiful. The other part of the club was at the bay, a mile down the road. There was a city of cabanas set around an enormous swimming pool, which Bailey helped to clean in the spring and fall. Beyond the pool, there was the beach. There were sailboat races in the bay. At the mooring, the masts pitching as the water moved, the sound of bells was continuous, bells tied high on the rigging and gaily sounding as the tide and wind moved the heavy hulls.

Bailey slipped down from the lion. The afternoon was so warm she cut across the golf course on her way to the bay. She might take a boat and row out into the sound of bells. She might even swim. At the bottom of the great front lawn, a line of huge trees had turned gold in the frost that hit last night and Bailey wondered, running towards them, why she was thinking thoughts for a second time and why she knew just where she would stop, excitement a pain in her chest, as she felt the magic aura wear away. "This has all happened before," she thought, as if there could be no plainer answer.

Tom and the Peabodys were playing the short fairway of the first hole, with Tom advancing quickly to the green. The fairway was a puny joke. Lots of players got a hole-in-one and even Tom made it in three shots.

As she stepped off the green a ball landed with a gentle bounce and stopped a few inches from the cup. Bailey reached up from the sand trap and gave the ball a shove. In a second, she was flat on her stomach again and hoping that Mrs. Peabody, and not her snooty husband, would get the benefit of her little boost.

"Congratulations, Polly. You've got yourself a hole-in-one."

"The hell I have! I'm going to give Georgie holy hell tonight! Her children are running wild."

"She's without a husband, my dear. Jack Bailey's been gone for almost a year."

"All the more reason she should manage her dreadful children."

"The little blondie is sort of cute."

"I can't separate her face from her accent, I'm sorry to say. Our poor Jimmy."

"I'm not following you, my dear."

"A cheap little trick like Cary Bailey is an attractive menace."

Dr. Peabody's piercing laugh sounded fagged as though it were an overused weapon.

"You know quite well," said his wife, "that boys like Jim don't go after that kind of girl – they fall into her trap. She's a slut!" Bailey had never heard such confident hatred. "Don't tell me you want Jimmy to marry her."

"Naturally, I don't. But for good old-fashioned reasons, Polly. I don't deny, as you do, that they're in love." Tom's sarcasm was sentimental compared to Dr. Peabody's scorn.

"I don't know why Cary loves our pathetic excuse for a son, but love him, she certainly does."

Bailey's ears, as the sound of their voices retreated, were a whirlpool of icy grief. Poor Cary!

The light of the sun lit up the moon's dead surface. Bailey ran like mad down the fairway, then rested and walked backwards. The roof of the clubhouse with its tall chimneys was a cruel city twirled by the indifferent earth through sun and shade. Her stone house was bullied by the pine trees. The highest branches hung over the roof and brushed the window screens as the wind blew. The sound was dreadful as she dashed up the walk to the kitchen door.

Cary was alone in the yellow kitchen, drying her rolled up hair in the oven. Bailey climbed up on the counter behind her and picked up a drumstick from the platter. There was no taste or smell as she chewed and swallowed, and no sound as the bone missed the garbage pail and fell by Cary's sneaker.

"Hey," her sister mildly protested as she closed the oven door. Her head was huge with pink hair-rollers because it was Saturday night and she was going out with Jim Peabody. Because she was always behind in her chores and her thick hair took so long to dry, Cary always had to bake her head. She looked so good in her jeans and soccer shirt. Thin and dark, she looked as good as Tom.

Bailey hated the hair-rollers and the tight ring of hair that Cary unlatched and felt to see if it was dry. She hated the dress and high heels she would change into.

"Why do you put up your hair when it's already curly?"

"It's too curly. Jim likes my hair neat."

Cary's vivid pride took away Bailey's control. Weeping, she jumped down from the counter.

"Hey, night owl, that thing with the golf ball wasn't such a crime." Cary hugged her. "You just played a trick."

Tom banged through the kitchen door, violently excited. "Dad's home, Cary. He's home. I saw his hat on the couch."

Rushing after Tom as he ran to the hall couch, Bailey stood next to him while he picked up the spruce felt hat. Lifting the hat from his hands she turned it over and touched the gold initials with her finger. S.P.

"Dad's in uniform, Tommy." Bailey pulled at her brother's back pocket while he knocked on the library door. "This isn't his hat."

Tom pressed his forehead and palms against the door. "Dad!" he shouted, "We want to see you too."

Georgie's voice jumped out of her. "Go away!"

"We want to see Dad, too!"

"For God's sake – go away!" Her rage was dreadful!

Tom kicked the door then flung Bailey to the floor in his dash for the stairs. Furious, she chased him to sock him but he was so miserable, hunched on Cary's bed, and so stupid. Tom knew as well as she that their father would come home from the war in his naval uniform.

"She didn't even tell us Dad was coming. We missed him too."

Sucking in her cheeks, Cary felt her hair under her red bandanna. Her large eyes watching Tommy were as plaintive as the wind that moved the tall trees outside the house. "She's his wife, Tommy. She missed him more."

"Bullshit!" Tom clenched his fist and waved it back and forth.

"Fucking?" Bailey laughed from the dim corner. "Is mother fucking?"

Inexplicable, violent, the revulsion of her beloved brother and sister overwhelmed Bailey. She turned to garbage and then to stinking fog as Cary and Tom loomed with cocked fists.

"That's not Dad's hat," she whispered.

Suddenly cheerful, Tom touched the ceiling in a splendid leap. "I'll have to quit smoking now and get back on the team. Watch out, Jim Peabody." Tom

grinned at Cary. "I'd like to see him messing with you now. And little sister here," he yanked her braid, "too bad you can't keep cutting school and sneaking off to the movies."

"Hey ho!" Georgie called out. At the sound of her footsteps on the stairs, Tom and Cary took a step towards each other and stared into the hall.

Georgie hung onto the door frame and panted for breath.

"Where's Dad?" Tom and Cary cried together.

Jack Bailey always said his wife had thoroughbred legs. Now, they trotted her stately trunk across the room to Cary's bed. Smoothing her pink sweater over her stomach, Georgie addressed them with slurred gravity. "Your father had hemorrhoids."

Cary looked desperately towards the door. "Can't he walk?"

"One's feet are not the usual site for – that – Cary,

dear." Georgie wagged her finger at her daughter. "I begged you not to drop out of college."

"Where is he?" Tom shouted.

"He's on his way home!" Georgie pressed her heart with both hands. "The Navy is sending him home."

"Quit the games, mother! Oh, God!" Tom's sick eyes sought Cary. "I just saw his hat on the hall couch."

Georgie was smug in her offering as though she possessed the last piece of a puzzle. "You saw a hat which looked like your father's, which is now gone."

Cary's face competed with her bandanna in its shade of red. "The man must have the same initials as Dad, then."

"S.P.? J.B.?" Georgie pursed her lips as she considered. "Sam Peabody, Jack Bailey?"

"A few little loops make all the difference!" Tom's miserable face was as red as Cary's. "Now don't they, mother?"

Georgie was puzzled by Tom's savage tone. "You're sore because he had no time to talk to you tonight. But tomorrow he's going to take us all up in his plane."

Georgie reached out for Tom's hands and swung them while her warm, melodious voice sang the pleasure of the coming day. Dr. Peabody owned the most expensive plane that could be bought. There was none of that dreadful vibration that made one want to vomit, and one traveled at a cozy altitude that didn't bury the details of the ground in height.

"I know how you love airplanes, Tommy. I was so thrilled when Sam suggested a spree."

Yanking away his hands, Tom spoke to the floor. "You promised Dad that while he was away you wouldn't go up in Dr. Peabody's plane."

"You're right!" Georgie joyfully embraced him. "What a wonderful boy you are, to remember such things." Tom's rigidity embarrassed her and she stepped back. "I'll call him now to say we can't fly with him – but don't you think it would be nice to take a drive into the country? It's such a charming airport. Before you children were born your father and I used to drive out weekends and just look at the planes. You can take your pad, Tommy," Georgie entreated the dark post that stood before her. "When you've drawn all you want we can have supper at some lovely country inn."

Georgie turned her pleading smile on Cary as Tom walked to the end of the room and took up a book. She sat down on the easy chair and put her feet up on the stool as she counted the days before Jack Bailey would be home. Monday, Tuesday, Wednesday, Thursday. To Bailey's amusement her voice was coming slower and slower.

If the slipcovers and curtains were shipped off to the cleaners the first thing tomorrow morning, if the floor people were called immediately, then everything could be accomplished by the end of the week. Georgie's voice got like mud talking; it was so thick and wet. Bailey leaned on the arm of the chair and stared into her mother's blinking eyes.

"She's off but still turning," she announced. "We'd better get her walking or she'll be here for the night."

As usual, Tom and Cary were so absorbed that they

didn't hear Bailey's monologue as she hauled her mother onto her feet and led her from the room. Georgie was obedient, and so light on her feet that Jack Bailey had been known to dance his comatose wife to bed.

Holding her hands, Bailey went backwards down the stairs. "Whoa, Bess. Easy girl, take it slow. Quit that, now! One hoof after the other. Just take it easy! Whoa, gal! Back out from there! Left hoof." Bailey stepped on her mother's foot. "Left, old Bess, Left! Good girl," Bailey cheered as Georgie sank onto her turned down bed.

After putting Georgie's glasses on her bedside table and tucking her hands inside the covers, it was Bailey's great pleasure to tote the bottle of whiskey that her mother had finished that night up to Cary's room and to pass it briefly between their downturned faces and their books.

Tonight the dark green bottle jutted up from her crossed legs as she sat in the easy chair and watched Cary dress for her date with Jim Peabody.

"Hemorrhoid," Tom read. "Venous dilation inside the anal sphincter of the rectum and beneath the mucous membrane. Gross!" He slammed closed the dictionary and leaned both elbows on its back. "But Dad's in the Pacific! How does Dr. Peabody know about it? Don't you think that's weird Cary?"

Cary sat at her dressing table and combed out her long, thick hair, "He is our family doctor, Tom. If he's got that thing then naturally Dr. Peabody would know about it."

"Why?"

"I've got to dress now." Cary glanced at the door.

"Why do you dress up for Jim Peabody? He'll be too drunk to know what you're wearing."

"Don't, Cary," Bailey cried. "You look so cool in jeans."

"And when the jerk spills gin all over you won't have to worry. The jerk!" Tom fumed.

Cary's caressing patience while she asked Tom to leave her room seemed as sad to Bailey as the sound of the doves hooting mournfully from the pine trees and the sound of the reservoir that dropped so far down the side of the dam.

"All that guy does is drink, Cary." Tom hung in the door, miserable with worry. "He flunked out of medical school; he sells eye-glasses to pay for his booze."

"His father forced him to go to medical school, Tommy. Dr. Peabody's a tyrant. You should hear the stories Jim tells."

"My bleeding heart!"

"You sound just like Dad," Bailey laughed from the chair and played an imaginary fiddle. Cary yanked her out of the chair and sent her sailing into Tom. As they plunged down the dark stairs, Cary slammed her bedroom door.

Chapter 5

"What a dump!" Tom scorned the country airport as Georgie locked the car. "You'll love Sam's plane, Tommy. Come along."

In her white trousers, Georgie walked to the hangar. Bailey looked at the tower made of criss-crossing iron bars. If she climbed it to reach the radar screen and sat on the platform, she'd be higher than the treetops.

Dr. Peabody jumped gracefully from the small plane. "Georgie!" He kissed her forehead and looked coldly over her head at the three children. "I'm flying a two-seater, damn it. I can't go up twice. I've barely enough gas to get down the runway."

"That's just where you're going to take me. Down the runway and back." Georgie turned to Tom with a satisfied smile. "I promised Jack to keep both my feet on the ground while he was away." Georgie tugged at Dr. Peabody's arm. "Don't worry about the children. They're wild to explore the woods and the river."

Inside the hangar, Cary and Bailey quickly grew bored with Tom's rage.

"There they go!" He imitated the whine of the plane's engine with a malignant face. "I hope they crash. I hope the motor conks out and they do a long, slow dive right in

Green Hill. That bitch! I hope she sees it coming for a long time." The coke machine rattled from his vicious kick. "I hope she dies."

"How would we get home?" Without knowing why, it delighted Bailey to make Cary laugh.

"Hook a ride in the ambulance." Tom made a snarling siren sound and looked sullenly through the narrow doorway. "Explore the woods, the river! It's scrub for miles and what river? If we got lost looking for it she'd just drive on home. "I forgot," he whined. "Don't blame me – I forgot."

Cary went to the door and stretched her arms into the bright sunlight.

"She's not that bad, Tom."

His deadly, condemning mood made Cary nervous. She took a cigarette from her jacket pocket. Tom lit it, took a puff then sat beside Cary on the bench by the door. "Dad will be home soon, Tommy. We'll be a nice respectable family again. He'll get mother off the booze and back to her thesis."

"Or else!" Tom smacked his palm.

The savage sound sent Bailey racing out the door. She wanted Tom to explore with her but he sat hunched and still on the bench as though in a cold, dark cave.

The radar screen slowly circled. Bailey hoisted up on the steel bars and began to climb. All the way to the top, getting narrower as they went, the bars cut radiant triangles of blue air. The radar was set on a little platform and Bailey wedged herself in.

Her legs hanging over, she gripped a bar in each hand

and leaned out over the countryside. Trees bent in the warm wind, the leaves flashing up their undersides. Birds flew beneath her and when Tom and Cary walked from the bench to the car they had the look of a game from her high perch. Their heads were the size of two dimes and the top of the car was a domino. At the end of the runway, the plane that Georgie was in could belong to Tom's collection of model aircraft.

Bailey slipped from the platform in a hurry then grew playful in her descent. The shadow of the tower grew fast as she killed time. It stretched out to swing over Tom, its shadow bars caging him up as he sat against the fence.

"What's the matter?" she cried. His distraught face was pink as the square she stood in.

"They've crashed," he whispered. "It's practically night and they're not back." He burst into tears.

"They've landed," Bailey grabbed his hand. "Come to the tower and I'll show you."

At a point in their climb, the tail of the airplane lifted out of the woods, scaring them. Its altering color as the sun dropped in the sky, the plane's mysterious pause, made Tom wild with nerves. It could not be them! They would come!

Dr. Peabody hurried Georgie across the macadam. Her head drooped and her feet turned inward and tripped her every few steps, while round her body, her crumpled white suit hung like dirty paper.

"Airsick," Dr. Peabody informed them.

Cary ordered Tom to the car. "Open the door," she yelled, then stepped up to Peabody. She took a tissue from her pocket and wiped the lipstick from under Georgie's nose. As she spat on the tissue she fixed her loathing eyes on Dr. Peabody's face.

"Your mother's not up to driving. I thought I could drive –"

"You get out of here." Cary stamped her foot. "My brother and sister are children and my father's in the war. You get away!"

Chapter 6

Tom wouldn't stop! He wouldn't let Georgie alone. In the car and now in the kitchen he repeated himself like a robot. Two hundred times he must have said as he was shouting now: "I don't care if you went up in the plane! I'm not going to report to Dad. I just want to know the truth."

Georgie pushed her teacup to the side with a doleful sigh. Her chin almost touched the table as she bent and peered at her face in the toaster.

"I need something!" she lamented. "I've run out of gin, it's too late for sin, beer is vulgar and besides I'm fat." Standing up, she turned her body sideways to the toaster. She winked at Bailey who was watching her with a smile and looked down at her stomach.

"I'm losing it. The dreadful battle of the bulge. Nobody wants a fat woman, but the heart stays lean."

Georgie was famous for her musical voice. It could charm the birds off the trees and never failed to beguile Bailey, who felt its vibrations in her scalp and the pit of her wrought-up stomach.

"Lean and hungry." Georgie swayed in front of the toaster. "But such is life and life is a disaster! Indeed, nobody gets out alive."

Her eyes flashed with alarm and shame as Tom punched her in the ass.

"Not my mother, dickhead!" Bailey attacked Tom's back, then his stomach as he turned in a rage. Doubled up, he gasped for breath. Georgie grabbed Bailey's hand and ran from the kitchen. As she pounded up the stairs, gas popped from her bottom.

Bailey handed her mother the key to her door. She watched the fumbling fingers then guided them, the key turning finally in the lock a second before Tom crashed against the door.

"I'll give you fifteen minutes without a drink, mother."

Bailey got her baseball bat from her closet and shouted through the door. "I'll kill you, Tom!"

"Ah, shit!" The doorknob rattled from his kick.

Georgie went on tiptoe to her bed and motioned to Bailey to come and sit beside her. She propped the pillow against the headboard and stretched out. As Tom kicked the door and cursed, she winked at Bailey and put her finger to her mouth.

"He's such a fool!" Bailey clenched the bat.

Two tears stood on the rims of Georgie's eyes. "I'm so miserable. No one but you knows how miserable I am."

"I hate Tom."

"Tom? It's so much worse than Tom." As though they'd been given permission the tears slipped down Georgie's cheeks. "I can only admit this to you, but I've been so happy since your father's been away. You children think he's so handsome but you don't have to see him naked. That huge thing of his – so mechanical, like a horse."

When her mother talked like this, Bailey concentrated on the soothing sound that was always to be heard at the back of her mind.

"You two fight so much," she whispered.

"He's always at me. Not a kiss, not a smile. He looks as though he's reading a book and there's that thing, like machinery in front of him. Sometimes I'm too tired or sick. Sometimes I'm thinking of Dad."

Georgie pressed her streaming eyes against Bailey's shoulder.

"Sometimes I fight back – you defended me."

Never unaware of the beauty of her mother's voice – shivers traveled her scalp and skin - Bailey was repelled by her body, which lay against her like a damp, hot rock.

"Tom's just like him. When I leave you, he'll be waiting for me. He's so snotty for fourteen. What right does he have not to believe me? He saw me get into the plane. He saw the plane taxi down the runway. He saw the plane take off."

"He's awful. He wouldn't listen to me at all."

"You weren't there!" Georgie moved away. "You were walking in the woods."

"I climbed the radar tower. I saw the plane at the side of the runway, pulled off to the side. You and Dr. Peabody came out of the woods and climbed back into it."

Bailey laughed at Georgie's aghast look.

"You're so funny, Ma. You should be on television."

"You didn't have your glasses on. You're blind as a bat without your specs," Georgie teased.

"Only when I read."

"Oh, no. You know what the doctor said. You only think you're seeing without your glasses."

"I get home runs all the time!"

"You're fresh." Georgie wrenched away and listened at the door.

Turning ugly in the freezing stream of Georgie's mysterious hatred, Bailey said very softly and slow, "why would I see you walking in the woods if you weren't?"

"Do you really think I'd take my new suit into the brambles? Think of that before you go running to your father." Georgie faced her, "Jack Bailey's a bum compared to my father. Dad was a great man and he loved me more than anybody or anything in the world."

Bailey removed her mother's clumsy hands from the key and let her out of the room. Tom sprang off the hall couch. As she locked her door, Bailey heard Tom start in again. He was not a spy for his father. He just wanted the truth for his own satisfaction. It was just so obvious that Georgie had gone up with Dr. Peabody. He wouldn't let her sleep if she didn't tell him! So, let her tell him!

Chapter 7

Bailey's welcoming salute to the Captain was languid. It was four o'clock. She lay in bed, lying back against her pillow, looking so decadent that her description of her increasing pollution appeared to be true. Talking in a lady's accent was packing her with poison.

"You," she told him, "are slowly killing me."

"I'm not killing you, darling. Subtract the content from your improved speech and you're almost ready for a marvelous future." Jim sat down at the desk and took up the history book with an excited smile. "Long, difficult but you've finished it in five days. You always remember what you read so your speed is a real improvement. It's wonderful, Bailey! Come on! You must agree that the change in your speech is a real break for your mind."

Bailey's dilemma was painful. It was a fairy tale that a boy as handsome and intellectual as Jim Peabody should acknowledge her mind. When they talked about the books he had her read, his respect for her opinion, often delight, was the deepest excitement she'd ever known. Then she agreed with him that the past, for all the quantity of forgotten time, had no more substance than a bad dream. Should blindness be regretted when one can finally see?

When words were a hostile code, Bailey had been

blind, bored and humiliated, and yet Jim's repugnance at hearing the speech of her childhood was so insulting.

At times during the day, she'd put her arms around her model house and peer in, watching the wings of the tiny glider as it turned on its string. Always it was turning, its movement like the trapped memory in Bailey's brain.

"Help," the girl whimpered, sinking into sleep.

Jim Peabody took Bailey's wool jacket from the closet and stood by the bed. What an excellent actress she was, to have made him see the corruption that was making her despair as she talked. Asleep, her look of sodden, spiteful prurience disappeared and Jim admired the adorable mobility of her melancholy face. A glance at the window showed Jim his image as well as the sunny afternoon. Commanding, distinguished, he looked very like the military photograph of his father that he always carried in his wallet.

An instant of intense energy electrified his body and filled the room with light. On the bed, Bailey was a golden figure, a princess, a belle, the passion of his life. Jim leaned on a bent knee and touched her shoulder with his fingertips. The warmth of her body shot up his arm, shot into his heart. Bailey's ugly view of herself was as external as her atrocious accent.

As he stared down at the girl, Jim felt the beauty of his masculine body in the weight and clasp of the military jacket and rejoiced in the strength of his will. One could break a horse or socialize a lovely woman with an intelligent, persistent routine. As a boy, he'd trained earthworms in a maze. Without doubt, given time, he could lead Bailey out of her vulgar childhood.

"Hey!" Bailey started from sleep at Jim's hard slap. Rubbing her thigh she smiled up at him with sleepy coquetry. On her feet now, she grumbled into her jacket that she was just horseflesh to the great Captain Peabody and it was cold, so cold!

Bailey woke up sullen against the evening wind. Huddled down in her jacket, she followed Jim blindly down the drive and onto the golf course. The autumn afternoon was ending. Trees blocked the slanted golden light and sent thin shadows across the narrow fairway. Plunging indifferently through stripes of sun and shadow, Bailey moaned that they'd miss supper.

Jim chuckled as he pushed her forward. Mrs. Hughes never let her cocktail and dinner go by and she was on the tee behind them playing the last hole. Looking back at the elderly golfer, Bailey snapped to life. She ran up on the green and watched Mrs. Hughes drive the ball.

"Thataway," she crooned as the ball bounded onto the green and rolled towards the flag.

"Come on, baby! In! In! In! Oh, no!" she groaned as the white ball stopped a few inches from the cup. Plucking the flag from the hole Bailey stood at a respectful distance as the dowager strode onto the green. She cheered as the short putt dropped in.

"Great playing, great shot! My brother plays golf. I know how hard it is. You almost got a hole-in-one." Grinning, Bailey replaced the flag. "You were so close, just inches. I had to stop myself from just whooshing it in."

Bailey's ebullience appalled Mrs. Hughes. Her friendliness at table, in the halls, her presumptuous association with Sam Peabody's son, constantly challenged the widow's conviction of social privilege. For cheapies like Bailey alcoholism was an outrageous indulgence. She despised the girl.

"If your little friend so much as touched that ball," Mrs. Hughes threatened Jim with harsh contempt, "I'd have given you both holy hell!"

Astonished at Jim's blatant fright, Bailey whispered that she hadn't interfered with the golf ball. Why didn't he tell her so? What was the matter with him?

"Tell her, Jim." Bailey poked his arm as Mrs. Hughes strode over the green then ran and stood in her path, her fists jammed on her hips and her legs in a wide stance. "I never would have touched a ball in play. I know better than that."

"I'd have given you holy hell."

The dowager's impermeable contempt seemed a mistake to Bailey. Her proud gaze was fixed a foot above her head, and had the girl jumping in the air to be seen as she cleared up this unjust interpretation. Jack Bailey, her father, was the manager of the most famous country club in the world. She knew all about golf – all the shots and rules, because he'd taught her. Her brother Tom was a golfer, too.

"You know I know how to behave, right?" Bailey's earnest eyes rejected the ridicule flowing from the iron heart of Mrs. Hughes; and her hands, in sudden persuasion on her shoulders, alarmed the imperious woman. The girl was passionate for acknowledgment.

"I don't know you at all."

"I'm telling you."

Fear flared in Mrs. Hughes's eyes, only to leave them deader than before. Disgusted, she turned on her heel.

"I'M BAILEY!" The girl hollered in pursuit then stood still in Jim's grip. "She wouldn't believe me."

"Believe who – for God's sake?" Jim was appalled at her presumption.

"Me!"

"Bailey by the Billion?"

"Me." The girl jabbed both thumbs to her chest. "Nobody else but me, Bailey."

"Oh, that's excellent, Bailey. That will get you far. Sweet Jesus!" He pushed her forward. "You're nothing to Mrs. Hughes. She can't separate your face from your accent."

"You said that?"

Jim glanced sarcastically at the empty space behind him. "Apparently."

"This has happened before?"

"That Mrs. Hughes set you straight?"

"He didn't like her," Bailey said, with mournful consideration. Yawning, she looked into the sun.

On the contrary, he liked her tremendously. Bailey was the only person he'd made a friend for so many years.

Against the wind, into the sun, huddled down in her coat, Bailey appeared to be listening with the top of her head. He liked her enough to see through the distortion of her past – what was her speech but the persisting sounds of a dead time? – and to cherish her beautiful spirit and her wonderful mind. Would she play a symphony on a fiddle? That was exactly the limitation of her accent to her increasing eloquence. Really, she was hearing not snobbery but the truth. If he was a snob, affectation and familiarity would warm him to her speech, but hearing her with Mrs. Hughes today he could only say with objective certainty that her accent was intrinsically ugly.

"It's true, Bailey, Mrs. Hughes doesn't know who you are, but that's not your fault." Jim stepped between Bailey's hunched figure and the wind. "We'll work and when we leave Stockbridge, all the important people of the world will bow down to you."

Jim felt such sweet compliance in her shoulders and in her arm as he walked her into dinner. He glanced at the setting sun. Following the low rays that ran through the swirl of her hair, Jim's heart leapt with love. Like scrubbing graffiti from a church wall, he was restoring the girl to her original dignity and she would be his wife. As vividly as before, a vision of his father as a young Army captain brightened the autumn evening to his eyes while his legs in the cold wind surged with energy.

"I know you!" Passing to their table, Bailey spoke loudly to his back.

Mrs. Hughes's presence, her hard, remote gaze, had the authority of metal to Jim as she looked up from the menu and said to Bailey, "By God, you'd better had."

"I DO!"

Rushing to their table, Jim was absorbed in choosing his dinner when Bailey sat down.

"I do know you, Jim. I remembered on the golf course. I had this insane feeling of repetition – a fit of it – and suddenly I remembered. You're the blond boy in my past. You sold me my first pair of glasses. I was with Tom."

"You're shouting!" Jim blocked her radiant eyes with the menu. "Eggplant's the vegetable tonight, Bailey. Shall I order for you?" Writing up the dinner order then signaling the waitress with the pad, Jim winced at Bailey's loud, crude voice, which was filling the ears of the region's most powerful and arrogant.

"Young lady," he nervously teased her, "you will never be successful in a drawing room until you learn to keep your voice down."

"When I was ten I made you my champion. I remembered on the green. I'm so excited, Jim. It's like knowing you in a past life. It's like reincarnation."

"Pipe down, please."

"You're the blond young man!"

Bailey's excitement was impenetrable to his influence and intensely embarrassing. Feeling Mrs. Hughes's disdain with all his nerves, Jim welcomed the big, blocking body of the waitress as supper was put down, and he immediately began to eat.

"I've remembered you, Jim. I'm so happy."

Jim resisted her eyes, which shone like a fairy story, and pointed to her cooling food while he again explained the social reality that made her memory of previous acquaintance a boring fantasy.

"Fantasy?" Bailey scraped the cheese off the eggplant and ate with clumsy indifference. "Memories are pictures of real things. Aren't they? I mean – the mind doesn't remember wrong."

"Your mind does."

"The feeling I had on the green, Jim – the feeling that

it had all happened before – I mean, I knew what Mrs. Hughes was going to say before she said it and when you said that she couldn't separate my face from my accent I felt this memory coming up, up, up and just before I got a picture the feeling stopped. God!" Bailey flung back in her chair. "But then when you stood blocking the wind and sun was on your face, this picture of you much younger zapped my mind. I met you when I was ten. God!"

Sweating in the pull of the dowager's malignant attention, Jim saw Bailey through her eyes and thought her radiant excitement moronic.

"What you think are memories, Bailey, are the fantasies of an alcoholic girl. Don't ever forget you were drinking, not living."

"Not when I was ten. You defended me!" Bailey fairly brayed.

"Speak like a lady!" Jim snarled, as Mrs. Hughes came by their table on her way from the dining room. When she'd passed, Jim lowered his contemplative gaze from the chandelier and found Bailey scarlet.

"Are you ill?" Appearing stunned, she wouldn't look at him.

"I think you're allergic to eggplant. Have you eaten it before?" Her progress was dense towards her room. "You're red as a tomato, Bailey – even your arms. The infirmary's the other way. Are you feeling too sick to hear me, Bailey?"

Bailey kept her face turned from him as she fished up her door key and put it in the lock. Her hair parting was rosy from the frightening pulse of her blood to her skin and he cringed at the heat his fingers felt.

"Allergies can be dangerous. Please let me take you to the infirmary."

"I'm not sick."

"You must be."

"I'm ashamed of my fantasies."

"It's not the eggplant?" Now Jim could look forward to the seven o'clock news.

Bailey looked up from the lock, her mortified eyes briefly on his. "I have fantasies, not memories. I should be horsewhipped."

Bending his head, Jim kissed her cheek. "It takes two people to make a memory, kiddo. It's a matter of agreement. Your family's just as silent as your model house. Really, darling – your past is a silent house – but your future is regal." Jim kissed her cheek again and pushed her gently into her room. "If you work."

"I thought you were in my past."

"I suppose it's a compliment that you stud your little soap operas with Peabody men."

Bailey's hollow moan, as if she really had become the cylinder of pornography she despaired of being, troubled Jim as he stepped into his room. It was certainly his duty to forbid his friend the debilitating comfort of fantasy, but he could not deny his joy at being, however mistakenly, the hero of her past.

In front of his mirror, with the memory of Bailey's adoring eyes, Jim stared at her version of himself – the handsome, upright, courtly youth – and felt for a moment the transformation of her delusion. Never less than

43

responsible and enduring, but spontaneous and bold – he looked a leader whom troops would follow. He took his father's photograph from his wallet and thrust his face close to the mirror while he compared the two images. For a moment the similar faces were both animated by the same commanding, intelligent spirit.

"Bailey," Jim whispered in helpless joy. To have mistakenly won the devotion of a noble child, was almost to have been a person who'd existed during that dismal time of his life beyond his conscious shame, and who'd been perhaps somewhat commendable. In a bound of hope, Jim was suddenly beyond his stubborn opposition to the girl's bogus conviction of a shared past. Only slowly, his optimism fading as reason returned, did he turn his back on the mirror and hang up the evocative jacket. He thought it strange to have taken such a flight, but stranger still was his aching regret, as he watched the evening news. For whom? He silently railed. For a fictitious person, some television type, a conception built on boredom and booze?

Astonished at the heat and wetness of his eyes, Jim leapt up from his chair and closed the bathroom door on the imperturbable television and Bailey's nightly noises beyond the wall. Running water in the sink, he stared into the cabinet mirror.

"But I don't cry," he informed his miserable face.

Jim Peabody hadn't wept for fifteen years and he felt a hundred and eight degrees from sorrow, felt rage, in fact, at his sudden susceptibility to Bailey's baloney.

"Knock it off," he snarled with quivering jaw. "Stop it, damn you! One of us has got to live in the goddamn world."

Chapter 8

"Hey guys. I have fantasies, not memories." Switching on the ceiling light, Bailey hurried to draw the yellow curtains across the two windows, the black glass mocking her shame before she could cover it up. Her desk and bed and dresser as she looked from one to the other were hostile witnesses, the dresser, especially, so contemptuously staring with its five sets of eyes.

"I was so happy."

First her sensation of vivid familiarity on the green with Mrs. Hughes and the younger, brighter face so transiently evoked by Jim's expression as he leaned towards her in the wind, had jumped her to a peak of joy. Contrary to his insistence that he'd been bleakly distant as a child, Jim Peabody was a knockout boy whose kindness had provided the only hope in Bailey's darkest years.

Selling glasses on a fall afternoon, Jim Peabody had become a fantastic figure to her, but the origin was human. She remembered the feeling of his fingers on her ear – and yet Tom had been so repulsive – talking to Mrs. Peabody as though the insulting woman were a family friend. Dismissing her fright, Jim hustled her into her room.

"You didn't really sell glasses?"

"If I had a job and didn't know it, then that makes me

an alcoholic like you. Cheer up, darling," he chuckled at the scarlet face. "All you need to do is a little work!"

"I'll work," Bailey whispered as Jim blew her a kiss from the door. Hope leaving through her knees, Bailey dropped to the rug. The happiness she'd felt as his boyish face emerged in her mind now was a torture of shame. With the reminder of her admiration came the sensations of the child she'd been – a good, honest child who passionately loved the beauties of her life. Who found nature and the feelings of her heart magical. A child Jim Peabody had met, had defended – oh, it was wonderful! But, he hadn't sold glasses – ever, ever, ever.

Bailey crawled to the closet and pulled the model house onto the rug. Usually, her solemn knowledge of the turning glider gave her the sensation of intelligent, kindly life. But tonight the retrieval of Jim's boy's face proved fantasy; she suffered the worst mortification of her stay at Stockbridge.

"How could I have told him? He was revolted to be in my past. He was so rude." The glider's look of reasonable persistence vanished and Bailey saw instead motion dependent on the tension of twisted string.

"I'm nothing," she whispered, weary of the futile pressure in her head. "I'm filthy fog from nowhere."

Chapter 9

There was a modest house made of stone. For many years a little girl lived there and her name was Bailey. Owned by the country club, it was always rented to the club's manager and enjoyed the magnificent view that restored the club members after their efforts at tennis and golf.

The stone house was lived in hard by the Bailey family. Their passions were contemporary and expressed in dreadful noise. Imperious, promiscuous, drunk, Georgie Bailey challenged her husband's authority and engaged her children in a troublesome intimacy. At night while the family slept, the rooms of the house endured the outrage as tradition commanded. The shame of the husband and the children's fear was absorbed in stoical silence until the previous year, when the child they all loved had gone.

In its two hundred years of life the house had never felt the like of Bailey's appreciation. In her joyful presence the manager's house had felt as grand as the clubhouse for all its antique grandeur and its sovereign hilltop site. Now the loom of its ornate bulk was resented as insult, even menaced as the child's exile continued from month to month.

Except for Bailey's bedroom, each night was passed in murmurous regret. No paint job, no repair or new decoration could touch the rejuvenation the child's return might bring. Inevitable as the coming dawn, the silence of the child's retreat frightened the other rooms to plead. Surely, as much as its neighbors, her bedroom must want Bailey back? Abuse rang in the steady silence. Loyalty to the human who sought its shelter was what distinguished a room from an empty box. What was the corner bedroom anyway, a square of brutish matter?

To suffer the injustice of gross misinterpretation was easier than the terror of the spoken truth. If it could, Bailey's bedroom would have its denunciation last until the dawn brought the shapes of the furniture out of the dark and the glider hanging from the ceiling turned from black to blue.

Day and night the glider slowly turned until the resistance of the wound-up string made it circle the other way. "Bailey," said the white letters down one of its sides. Each wall was silently informed as the glider spun.

Whether it was filled with sun, or the pearly light of an overcast day, the room enjoyed the memories that the revolving name brought forth – the child's short life played like a movie on its four walls.

But at night, the slow circling of the glider was unnerving; the waves of its movement broke on the walls of the room like the obstinate impulses of an obstructed memory. For all the dark repetition there was such effort. Such fear. The dawn was respite. The parade of noisy hours, the quick shadows of birds on the walls cheered the room. Only in the late afternoon did it regret the laws that sent the earth and glider spinning.

No, it didn't want her back.

The pain of memory was enough to fear; but to actually feel again the misery that seeped off the child as she turned on the television set, and – gulping vodka from her stashed bottle – welcomed another afternoon on Bailey Street, was as dreadful to anticipate as an attack of fire.

The soaps, the family shows, even the cartoon characters, had a house on Bailey Street, and living in them were the members of her family. Their attempt to confuse her with their various disguises and different voices was futile. The vodka gave her x-ray vision and, in a flash, beneath freckles, a beard or black skin, she found Tom, Cary and her parents.

"I love them and they love me," she'd drunkenly tell the corny screen. "I'm the happiest girl in the world."

Chapter 10

"Ah, Captain Peabody, too harsh, too hard." Cozy in her unmade bed, Bailey gently grumbled as "the animal trainer", her current name for her only Stockbridge friend, clicked off the cartoon show that she'd been watching on television. Jim held up the history book that he'd assigned for the week's reading.

"It's time to work, kiddo."

"Take it out, Captain! I've finished *The History of the Massachusetts Bay Colony*. I'll talk about Cotton Mather if you let me suck it and sit on it. I know your reputation. I know what a great man you are, but the days you made love to me I reduced you to your cock. It's such a soft, blind thing when it first lies in my hand – then watch out! So hot, Captain! So hot and hard! Ride me! You must! I'm dying for a ride."

"Why must you talk like that?

As quiet as the front of his trousers and sweetly melancholy, Bailey's gaze lifted to his face. "I told you when I talk like this, the way you want me to talk, that's the way I talk."

"And I tell you," Jim responded cautiously to the dull directness of her eyes, "respectfully, I submit to you,

Bailey, that your wonderful new accent is not intrinsically linked to pornography."

"Submit your dick, Captain Sammy. Hell's bells, I'm crazy for a touch."

"Hell's bells?" Jim gently mocked her.

Bailey turned over on her stomach and fell asleep with a moist, crumbly laugh. Gone with the girl's consciousness was the perplexing alteration of her personality. Whenever Jim's ears delighted in the reformed refinement of Bailey's speech, he was visually distressed and mystified by his impression of a lewd and spiteful obesity, which, as much as himself, depressed the newly accomplished girl. It was as if, to Jim's relief, a greasy mist obscured the modest, intelligent, noble face which sleep had restored.

What could he believe but the girl's own description of her current torture – that speaking like a lady made her feel like a slut? But, surely he must focus more on the transience of this phenomenon than on the pain it was causing poor Bailey. Her loyalty to her unclaimed past, some guilt perhaps, was demanding its due. But the girl was a fighter and could endure this trial for the sake of a glorious future. He regretted her despondency and the physical lethargy, which felt to her like the past in dismal return. But he would continue to admonish, prodding her alert. Hail the "animal trainer."

On a December afternoon, at the end of their walk, Jim kept pushing Bailey from a stall. "Come on, pal, we need pace for this cold."

"I was so happy – right over there. It was just before supper on that brick path when I remembered the blond young man. I was never going to be unhappy again."

She'd be plenty unhappy. Jim punched her spine whenever she reverted to her old accent. Just then, had she realized her regression? Taking her wrist, pulling her along, Jim lectured over his shoulder. With his father so soon arriving for his Christmas visit, Bailey had to sharpen up. The future daughter-in-law of the nation's most celebrated surgeon must appear to be qualified for the honor and would be – Jim raised his fist – if Bailey's body became a carpet of bruises.

"I like a handsome man to use his fists, first his fists and then his iron dick." Hating Jim, Bailey strained to keep hold of his slippery jacket. "Bruises make me dark as them. "My sister, my brother, Cary and Tom," Bailey mourned in vulgar tone, then stopped and received Jim's corrective blows on her patient back. Her drowned memory was sending up debris – the belongings of her brother and sister were the briefest visions behind her closed eyes. Cary's red bandanna and the old convertible that Tom drove with such punkish vanity; Cary's clothes, her soft wool sweaters and skirts; her huge plastic hair rollers – all debris from the lost wreck of her past.

"I was so happy to remember you." Bailey pressed her temples then flung a gesture at the grey woods. "It was like children meeting in such fright, your fingers were so warm on my ears and you said to Tom that I told the truth!"

Interrupted by Jim's menacing look, Bailey was confused in her intensity and then speaking "properly" amended her offence.

"Memories are like stories: He said, she said ... mood. Who cares?" With a pretty gesture and a wink, Bailey took Jim's arm.

"You're handsome enough in your own way. You don't have to be the god I thought I'd remembered. So what if the light-switch is off in there," she bumped his side. "And out there and everywhere – but so what? Only kids need to be happy. For me it's enough to sleep, eat and move my bowels. Hell, Captain, doesn't your famous philosopher say that life, the very stuff of life, is but a dream? But I really must insist on the starch and grease. When I was a child I loved raw bacon."

Stopping, Bailey withdrew her arm from Jim's and clutched herself in a sudden glow. "I did eat raw bacon – just the fat. What?" She smiled at him with sparkling eyes. Imitating his gesture, his finger to his lips. She laughed explosively at such an honest emergence of the past. For who'd make up raw bacon? Not even Bailey by the Billion. Raw bacon was the real McCoy.

"Ow!" Unguarded in her excitement, Bailey clutched her aching arm and surprised Jim with a kick. "What's your problem?"

"Can't you remember?"

"Yes!" she rejoiced. "There's no raw bacon in television land."

"My father's coming in two weeks and you haven't learned to hear yourself. When you switch from the well-bred, intelligent girl to the little cheapie and you don't know it, how can you possibly eat luncheon with father? It's a disaster!" Jim lurched away.

"I'll suck raw bacon and purr along like royalty." Humiliated but terrified of the jeering sky, Bailey trotted to keep at Jim's side. "I'll be divine. I'll bring your father out with divine questions. I'll inquire after your penis, Jimmy. I'll wonder with my hands so prettily moving and my radiant smile if your father might sew it back on – as a wedding present, don't you know. I'll be charming and thin, because tonight it's back to vegetables and fruits and Captain, ferocious exercise. Nothing burns off calories like playing tennis in the cold." Well spoken. Chipper, she'd reward him for all his work.

"Really," she curtsied before passing through the door that he held. "I know how to behave."

"You can't stop the sex talk – you've said so. Obviously, you can't meet father." Bitterly disappointed, Jim left her behind in the dreary corridor.

Chagrined by his presence, yet panicked alone, Bailey sped after him with a pounding heart. Certainly she could control her mouth. What went in, what came out, no problem, man. Just let her shelter in the insult of his company – oh, please!

"Insult of my company?

"You don't like me."

"If you don't know by now that I like what you could be, then you're stupid and I shall eat my dinner alone."

"But if I don't know what I've been – "

"Be thankful," he interrupted her anguish, "and shut up."

"Isn't he masterful?" Bailey blushed as she clung to his arm, her feet doing double time to his swooping stride. "Could any man save more time for the human race than Captain Sammy? Mrs. Hughes wants his time – oh, wow! First nod, then rod. Oh, juicy."

Jim's voice was cruel in her ear as he sat beside her at dinner. His name wasn't Sam if she didn't mind. Not his father, not her blond young man, he was only who he was.

"You're wonderful," Bailey grieved in her warm, social tone. "No one understands history like you do, Jimmy, or talks about it so beautifully. You could be Secretary of State when your father dies."

"I'll be ready for it."

"And I'll be perfectly proper."

"Or else." Raising his water glass Jim toasted their future, with pinched joy.

Chapter 11

Two days later, Jim stood up to hold Bailey's chair as she walked into the dining room. She looked spruce from the neck down in a new yellow sweater and gray slacks. Her melodious greeting began the third morning of her promise to maintain the proprieties.

"I was going to wait until the end of the day, Bailey, but really, I'm too pleased. Should I be pleased, or should I be angry at the verbal stubbornness that's curled my hair for months and months?" He grinned with happy pride.

"Should I rebuke you for unnecessary torture? Come on, kiddo," he laughed as Bailey yawned, "admit you feel better speaking like a lady." He looked over at Mrs. Hughes, who read the newspaper in a dome of gloom. "Now we can all play golf together, How about it, darling? Shall I set it up this morning?"

"I love you, Jimmy. You're a rope thrown into my swamp, but today I can't play golf – I'm just too exhausted."

"You look marvelous."

"Not the face I washed this morning. My eyes look like rotting lilies and I long for dark glasses. While you frolic with Mrs. Hughes, I shall be back in bed."

Shaking her head at Jim's inadequate description, the

waitress declared that if Bailey had been flattened by a two-ton truck, the girl could hardly look worse. Even Mrs. Hughes wondered if early winter flu hadn't taken its toll on his depraved young friend. Surely, Jim should alert the sanitarium's physician.

Gratified by the dowager's concern and hopeful of its increase, Jim gravely announced Bailey's problem to be emotional.

"Emotional? Oh, dear!" Mrs. Hughes hurried outside to her game, her annoyance a setback to Jim's diplomacy.

"When she speaks as I insist she must, she feels guilty," Jim explained.

"For presumption?"

"To her background."

"Bizarre." As though informed of animal habits, Mrs. Hughes's titillation was mild and so quickly forgotten in the preparation for her drive that Jim felt shamed in his sympathy for Bailey then confused by a searing hatred for the dowager as she knocked off a long, true ball.

When Bailey didn't show up for lunch, Jim thought the manner of the waitress accusing, but immediately on opening her bedroom door he rejected the guilt that engulfed him – the room was a goddamn bog of inappropriate emotion. Tossing up the windows, the stench of melodrama drifted into the clean winter air and Bailey, in bed, disturbed by the freezing drafts, began to weep. Heaving up, she pointed at her model house. "The glider's moving in there, Jim. It can't stop because of its twisted string. Isn't that sad?"

"You can't really expect me to sympathize with a

lifeless object." Her shoulders and arms were humble under his directing hands. She must get up, wash her face and begin the afternoon's work. "My brain's so cold and my body is lonely. My poor, dear abandoned house." On her knees, Bailey flung her arms around the model. "I'm sorry for you – darling glider."

"You made the glider, kiddo. Who do you think you're talking to?"

Bailey put her ear to an upstairs window. "Cary cries so much."

"Young girls always weep."

"Over bastard boys,"

"What?" He menaced her with slowly closing fingers.

"You're Cary's Jimmy." You're the Peabody bottle of gin."

"I've forbidden you to equate our experience." Jim lost his breath as Bailey's eyes remained on his, in intolerable challenge.

"The blond young man is a bum! My poor sister."

"What does it take to re-train your pathetic mind? I've had the patience of Job, Bailey, but it's run out."

She looked at him calmly as his fist struck her shoulder, then walked to the bed and crashed onto her stomach. "My poor sister – you were so drunk."

Jim's rage swelled in the absence of her eyes and slinging his leg over her rump, he harshly posted while he punched her soft back.

"You will learn, learn, learn," he panted.

"Do it, Sammy. No one does it like you do. Get hard, get huge and hot! O, dear Dicky, do. Mount me! MOUNT ME!"

"The name's Jim, you moron!"

"Get me off," Bailey whined as his blows fell. "Pound me, piss on me, oh, please, please, please!"

Hitting harder and harder, Jim felt the reverberations of his correcting fists pass up his arms with intense pleasure. Bailey's drowsy groans imparted to his body an irresistible attractiveness, a potent, correct, vitality that increased with the force of his fists on her lazy flesh. He felt the serene pride of a magnanimous superiority and an astonishing warmth of blood.

'STOP! STOP! JIMMY! PLEASE!"

He heard her change, her urgency, but the rightness of Bailey's beating, the deep, whistling purpose, like an arrow flying to the mark, was not to be interrupted and Jim hit on in growling thrill until Bailey, with a desperate cry, bucked hard and slung him to the floor.

His eyes locked on her, and he was swiftly on his feet. Sitting now, Bailey fell back on her elbows and raised her legs. "Wake up," she pleaded. "You must."

"You're the one in dreamland," He socked the soles of her feet with deft fists. "I'm the teacher, remember? Remember?" The sudden redness of her face, the astonishment, then quick pity in her eyes, were confusing. He followed her eyes to the front of his trousers.

"I don't have erections," Jim softly announced. The strain of the flannel material was considerable. "I can't — that's why I'm here."

"Poor Jimmy."

Bailey's soft, sad eyes aroused the most terrific shame and Jim lunged at her with finger pointing.

"You will not think that I was an alcoholic like you. You will not, Bailey. I am not your blond young man."

His violent gesture in Bailey's mirror caught his eye and panting he stared at his waist. "But I don't feel anything, he whispered. "I don't understand."

The army jacket looked arbitrary and drab as though he'd been dressed by a correctional institution. What's happening?" he appealed to the girl. Her quiet sympathy fanned his shame to torture. Ripping open the musty jacket, he slung it onto her lap.

"This is your fault – your swamp," he covered his erection with his hands. "Oh, god," he moaned when his lungs drew in raucous air. "I'm crying but I never cry – SHIT."

As he grabbed up the jacket, tears flowed down his cheeks. "This is your pornography that I've gotten into. You're dangerous kiddo. You should wear a sign. GODDAMN IT! I've got to get out of here."

"Poor Jimmy."

"I hate your ugly, poor man's accent."

With sweet insurrection Bailey studied his face and said, in the voice of her birth: "Tough shit, man!"

Chapter 12

Why was it raining? Late December, Christmas right on them and yet, it was pouring again.

Every other year, in the attic's memory, it had snowed by this time. Nature was so queer these days. Something dreadful was going to happen. As they had for a week, when Cary's room had first expressed its distress, the other rooms waited for the library to relieve their growing fears. That all the books in the house should be shelved in one place induced as much resentment as respect and usually the house so quelled its curiosity that to hear its musical voice in answer to a question was the library's greatest pleasure. Now, its silence seemed as ominous as the attic's repeated refrain.

Mr. Bailey had been home for two weeks. In the old days he would have fixed the roof the first thing, but he'd done nothing but read. He seemed to have exchanged his turbulent features for a single expression of kind bewilderment. He'd grown chaste and endured Georgie's unabated rage with an astonishing placidity.

The master had stopped drinking and was indifferent to Dr. Peabody's usurpation of his wife. Physically and financially, the club, at his return, was quite a mess, but while he supervised the remedies with a disinterested efficiency, he completely ignored the havoc of his own house. Used to his sturdy maintenance, the rooms were aghast. They could only listen while mechanically, compulsively, the attic vented its anxiety. When the plaster crashed down from Cary's ceiling, the house went off like a bomb. Howls of fear endorsed the attic's dreadful prophecy: the sun and the master's normal self would never come out again!

Bailey's bedroom wondered at the library's silence. Over the years it had read itself to rationality and battled with the supernatural in whatever forms the other rooms chose to dread it. When unusual weather caused whimpers, the library quoted the Farmer's Almanac until calm was restored. Why did it not say at once that in the past one hundred years it had rained on Christmas as much as it hadn't? Why was it not assuring the others that the present storm was no freak of nature and therefore completely unconnected to Mr. Bailey's mysterious change?

In the growing hysteria, Tom was in the blackest mood of his life. In school the kids thought he was very strange. He got into fights at the drop of a hat, but mostly he cut to go drink at the movies or in the fields behind the school. And look what the sinister weather was doing to Bailey. She'd thrown Tom's birthday present in the garbage can. For weeks, after school, she'd been putting on her Wave uniform to admire herself for an age in the bathroom mirror. Suddenly, it was in the garbage. It had to be the rain controlling her. The house could never remember it raining on Christmas. It was the end of the world.

Bailey's room was also terrified, but of voicing its opinion, not of the prolonged spell of rain. Overflowing toilets, the plaster falling down from Cary's ceiling —

physical things – roused it to a state of mild anxiety, similar to the panic that took over when it forced itself to speak.

The kitchen called for quiet, then the dining room did. Gradually the rooms understood that it was not the rats in the cellar, nor the shriek of the pantry pipes, but Bailey's room desperately jetting along.

Lie? Was the downstairs hall hearing it right? A lie had caused this trouble? Caused the rain?

Questions were so much easier than talking from the blue and Bailey's room relaxed. Was Georgie a witch, she laughed, to cause the rain? Obviously, she and the storm were disconnected, but certainly it was her fault that the children were so ruined – especially Tom. The entire year Jack Bailey was away the children thought he was in the war. They thought he was an officer in the Navy, the pilot of a fighter plane. Georgie had told them that, when in truth, their father was in Stockbridge Sanitarium, drying out.

At last the library spoke. The delightful voice calmly ventured among the groans, the murmurs and deep sighs. It was true that Georgie had not told the children that their father was an alcoholic, but the fact that they'd been living a lie all that time was plainly wrong thinking. In the minds of the children, for a wholesome year, their father had lived as a fighter pilot. Like mollusks secreting pearls around tiny, foreign objects, the months that the children had believed in this heroic idea of their father were precious jewels, whose influence, both backwards and to the future, could not be reversed. Could this possibly be the definition of a lie?

Always, Bailey's room had felt that it was not respect for the library's brain, but the ache of its own ignorance, which rushed it to agree with the library along with the rest of the house. Whenever the library spoke, its ears were filled with its own voice, despairing that it didn't understand. Now the beguilement of a picture – three glistening pearls – strengthened its suspicion that the library was full of it. The three pearls were really splinters in the three wounded minds.

"The children are sick," shouted Bailey's room. "They didn't defend their father. They thought he was a hero, that he'd throw Dr. Peabody out of the house like garbage. Tom, especially, kept picturing the day when his father would bound up the walk from the taxi and just pitch out Peabody, like trash. The whole year the kids kept quiet, kept to themselves and didn't make a row. They didn't know that their father was so shrunken and subdued that pansy Peabody, sitting out the war, could have blown him over. The kids would have struggled too, if they'd known that their father was shaking like a leaf and wore slippers all the time. Now, they can't look at him. That kind, bewildered look makes them ill with pity and guilt and that's because they were told a lie. It was a lie!"

The other rooms were moved, but very nervous. It was only seconds after the library launched its reply, that their minds went blind with the need to endorse the idea that if Jack Bailey had died in the sanatorium or had followed his wife's plan and worn a rented officer's uniform, the good effects of Georgie's story would have gone on forever. All the rooms but Bailey's eagerly agreed that if Jack Bailey had worn the damn costume, in the three minds of his children, the truth of his heroism would have reigned until their deaths!

Chapter 13

"That perfect idiot! She's signaling left and going right. Aren't they the worst, Bailey, these woman drivers?" Georgie grinned over the high collar of her fur coat. "Marlborough Street? Hells bells, that's it!" Bailey stifled a scream as Georgie, hauling on the wheel, cut across two lanes. "Is that fool honking at me? Honk, honk! You geese, you stupids! Damn it! God damn it all to hell! Georgie lifted her foot from the brake and looked down at Bailey, who'd been thrown to the floor of the car.

"I've got a wheel up on the ramp because of grafters and two bit pols getting rich off these hairpin curves and there you are with a fever – a high fever, fooling around on the floor. Put it in reverse, that's it. Then back slowly and carefully off the ramp. Hang on, engine!"

"Oh, valiant Detroit! It's true the country's vulgar, but don't tell me America doesn't know how to make things. That wall is a half a foot high, but so what? Detroit's tough."

Georgie put her hand on Bailey's knee and kept pressing it as she gloatingly described the horrors of their life had they missed the Marlborough exit. Captives of this damn river drive, the next bridge would have spun them over the river to Charlestown where the tiny, choked streets led irresistibly to the slum district. Where under the elevated trolley tracks, black men hunched in the bitter wind and glared. Where garbage blew.

"Who pays the highest taxes in the country? We do!" Georgie's light fist drummed on Bailey's knee. "Higher than California we pay – and yet the city can't put up a decent road sign. I saw it in time, thank God. I always see it, but your father goes back and forth over the river like a lost soul. Oh, Bailey! Can you believe he's coming home tomorrow?"

Bailey slammed to the floor again as Georgie hit the brakes. Working the car into the short space, she was soon panting as she criticized Bailey's muted acceptance of this great event.

"What did you say? Big Daddy Boom Boom comes back? Because of the bombs, is that why you call him that? I never said he was a bomber, you know."

As Georgie slipped across the front seat, her determined eyes fixed on Bailey's face, Bailey vigorously pointed at the deep puddle that she wished her mother to avoid. Soaking her boots, wetting her trousers, Georgie was indifferent as she tramped along to the doctor's office. The only reason that Georgie would refer to Jack Bailey as a bomber was if he was one. But he was not, which made it an impossibility, didn't Bailey see, that she should ever have called him one. Big Daddy Boom Boom? If not to describe the work of a bomber, what did the nickname mean?

"Boom, boom!" Bailey lightly boxed her mother's arm as they walked. "I hate his coming home! I hate your fights!"

"There are no marriages without words, Bailey. Ow! What are you hitting me for? Stop it, damn it!"

Bailey caught Georgie's hand and shouted, "Dad's words made you black and blue – but you don't stop him."

"You don't have a fever." Georgie felt Bailey's forehead. "I'm afraid you're just obnoxious."

As Georgie sped away, Bailey thrust up her chin and opened her mouth as though she were strangling. Her frustrated eyes caught the sharp look of an elderly man and she closed up, very quiet and grim, and began to run.

"Your mother's in with the doctor." The nurse hurried her down the hall and into an office with dark green walls. It seemed to Bailey as she took the long white robe from the nurse that her mother and Dr. Peabody were much further away than the end of the room. As the nurse unzipped her jacket, Bailey felt them as small, fierce animals about to fight. Pulling off her undershirt, she saw Georgie coming at her and she backed away.

"I'm your own mother, for God's sake."

Dr. Peabody's shrill laugh made Bailey shiver. "It's a modest age, Georgie – for children."

Shaking down a thermometer, Dr. Peabody indicated with a harsh dip of his head that Bailey should sit herself on the examining table. While he waited for the thermometer "to cook" he chatted with Georgie and informed Bailey with his cold and caustic gaze that her existence was a nuisance.

When he sat up beside her on the table and put the head of his stethoscope all over her chest and back she felt her commonness repelling him and she hunched her shoulders in apology.

"I'm sorry," she mumbled whenever she had the chance.

"The difference between this one and Cary is amazing." His long fingers closed on her thigh. "What does she do with it?"

Georgie looked adorable as she thrust up her fists and challenged him. "She boxes."

"That's an ugly sport for a girl." His distaste made Bailey sorry for her mother. "Why do you let her do it?"

It was doubtful she had mononucleosis – her color was too good, but she must be tested out all the same. Dr. Peabody rubbed her finger with alcohol, jabbed the tip with a needle then sucked a tiny line of blood up the length of a glass tube. He corked it and as he sucked at the tip twice more, Bailey looked out at the dark, green walls. Her dread of school dropped away and her relieved heart pumped joy through her body as Dr. Peabody, his voice as dry as the winter sun, informed her mother that a week or two in bed, possibly more, was his immediate prescription. He'd know more when the blood test came back from the lab, but something was up, for Bailey had a temperature of a hundred and one.

Dr. Peabody tapped her shoulder. He was going to talk to her mother in his office next door. Bailey was to get dressed and go back to the waiting room where her mother would quickly come.

"Don't worry," his cold eyes annulled her, "we're going to peg this thing down and you're going to have a wonderful Christmas."

Christmas! Her horror of school had steadily grown

since September, until the present had become a torture chamber. The two remaining weeks before Christmas vacation threatened so drastically with moments of humiliation that Santa on the street corner, the decorated trees on the Common, seemed less like the future than a dim, cherished memory. From the beginning of the school day to the afternoon dismissal, Bailey fought down panic as her broken mind limped through the day. But Christmas was coming! It was coming!

Bailey pulled on her sweater and took the stethoscope from the drawer of the examining table. Hopping up, she imagined Dr. Peabody's bright shoes as she crossed her ankles. Pressing the nozzle against the green wall, a feeling of great seriousness swept over her. She spoke coldly to the wall. Its heartbeat had stopped, but never mind, they would get it going again before Christmas.

Examining the wall as carefully as Dr. Peabody had gone over her chest, she heard voices mysteriously stretched and alternating, high and low. Tracking the sound to behind the desk, she faintly heard her mother and Dr. Peabody talking. She sat down on the swivel desk chair and softly turned herself to this crucial examination.

Dr. Peabody was excited and upset. Bailey listened intently. That was amazing but yes, it was so. He sounded harsh and unhappy while Georgie was soothing, as soothing as she was to Tom. Each one said "Jack" and "Stockbridge" more than they said anything else.

The nurse was at the door. Bailey jumped down from the table and put the stethoscope back into the drawer. Apologizing as she followed the nurse into the waiting room, she felt her knees grow cold as Georgie's words made sudden sense. Cary was pregnant! Could she have possibly heard that?

"I could hear through the walls with that thing."

"I'm not surprised." The nurse sat down at a desk and opened a large, green book.

"You're not?" Bailey's heart thumped.

"The walls are as thin as paper here. Mrs. Cleary wants to bring in Billy but there's not a thing until after Christmas." Bailey went to the window and stared out into the rain. Christmas was again as distant as the moon and the present was an icy, dark place of sin where Cary was somehow managing to live. As Georgie put her coat around her shoulders and Bailey followed her out of the office and back along the street to the car, her body was again just the hideous place where her heart pumped and her lungs blew.

Even the rare appearance of Georgie's best mood, the funny way she tried to get the lipstick off her teeth and then drove into the wrong street, the stream of compliments as she looked vigorously around to get her bearings —Bailey's ears should be burning at what Dr. Peabody said about her, what a beautiful girl she was, what a star she was going to be whenever she picked up a tennis racket – but even compliments could not draw off her fear.

Georgie threw her arm past Bailey's nose as she braked the car. There was the old school! Perched on the steep hill, it was the narrow brick building to which she and Polly Peabody had walked every morning for twelve years.

"We had an hour of singing every day and until the sixth grade you had to unroll your mat on the floor after lunch and take a rest. Ever since, I've missed my mat, which is why I think I'll begin yoga. Polly says you bring a towel and lie on a soft carpet. When you aren't holding up a leg," Georgie leaned towards Bailey with a tortured look, "you nestle on your stomach with your cheek turned to the side, just as we did at dear old coffin for twelve blissful years."

"I heard through the wall with the stethoscope," Bailey whispered. "I heard you say that Cary was pregnant."

Georgie tugged her braid and pinched her cheek with warm delight. "A spy, you know, has to be one hundred percent sure. It's no bloody good just being ingenious. A stethoscope?" She pulled Bailey's ear. "How the hell did you think of eavesdropping with a stethoscope?"

"I wasn't spying," Bailey wept. "I was just playing Dr. Peabody and I heard you say that Cary was pregnant."

Georgie yanked on the handbrake and opened her arms. Bailey's face rode her laughter as her head was kissed and fondled.

"Are you absolutely sure you didn't hear me say to Dr. Peabody that Cary was phlegmatic?"

"You did say that?" Bailey hugged her. "You really did? I'm so happy. I was so scared."

Soothing Bailey's face with her cheek, stroking her shoulders, Georgie hummed and chuckled, then violently flung her away as she whirled round and shouted at a honking car to go to hell. She settled herself down to drive.

"The nerve!" she panted.

Did Bailey remember these streets from the days when

73

Grandma was alive? Did she recall the Sunday lunches and the long walks that they were forced to take? Bailey got up on her knees to look at the hilly, old-fashioned streets where her mother had been a girl.

Georgie drove slowly by the tall houses with carved doors and asked Bailey, in the tone of an intimate friend, whether she didn't agree with her that Cary was phlegmatic about Jim Peabody. Didn't she agree that in Cary's case, the kiss of the handsome prince had put her to sleep? Once charming and bright, their beautiful Cary was sadly transformed. How could she go out with a young man who was always drunk and then keep on dating him? Could Bailey please explain what it was in Cary's character that in contact with the male sex turned her into a dread lump?"

"It's this female thing," Georgie smiled easily into Bailey's shocked face. "It's the spine of every religion in the world – the martyrdom of women. I escaped it. I bet dollars to doughnuts that you have." Georgie swept the car onto the river drive. "So please tell me what the hell has happened to Cary?"

Bailey's leg muscles began to ache with confusion. These exciting times with her mother were rare and yet what Georgie had said about Cary was so frightening and sad. Watching the crowded road, she could feel Georgie's look on her cheek, mourned its removal, yet was a thousand miles from a thing to say.

"It's a very queer thing about Cary and me. When I'm reading and hear the vacuum going or savor the delicious smells of her cooking, I think, my God, I'm living in her generation and she's living in mine! Look, Bailey! The college is so lovely reflected in the water. No matter how many times a day I drive this road that sight always thrills me. But Cary dropped out. That paper she did on Hegel was distinguished – ah, I don't get it. Do you?"

The towers of the university, the brick dormitories – a charming city of them, were just as thrilling as her mother said, and Bailey remembered her joy the day that Cary got accepted. She'd danced about the room, clicking her heels, only to see slowly that Cary was indifferent to the letter. She was expected to go, so she would, but she didn't want to, and frankly, her imagination would have to stretch to the point of pain for her to see Bailey ever walking in the college yard.

The memory of that conversation made her feel sick as they drove quickly along: she stared at the smooth water that drowned the details of the college scene the way that pain seeped into time and finally went away.

Cheerfully lamenting, Georgie drove round and round the Common looking for a parking space. It was outrageous, preposterous and insane that to complete the last cinchy duty of the day, she was forced to park two miles away from the liquor store and hike. She would not! She would double park and leave Bailey in the car.

"You look so miserable, darling."

Bailey recognized her mother's radiant mood without feeling its warmth.

"Cary used to be so wonderful."

"You know that," Georgie gripped her shoulder, "and I know that. The Peabodys suppose that Cary's morbid condition is a compliment to their son. His attractiveness, they think, has stricken her dumb. They're in love with themselves, you see. The old name, his current fame. They're overwhelmed by their liberality at the thought of presenting my daughter with a bottle of Peabody gin. Well, I won't allow it! Oh, no! If it gets so far as the church, you'll see me on my feet, you'll hear me loud and clear with the reason why they should not wed. More liquor than blood in his veins, your honor!"

"A bottle of Peabody gin," Bailey laughed. "How can Cary love him so much?"

"She's desperately in love with him for the same reason that she can't love him." Out of the car, Georgie extravagantly slammed the door. "She doesn't know him."

Bailey slid behind the wheel and watched Georgie zip between the slow-moving cars. Her legs moved nimbly and looked so thin beneath her heavy trunk. With a toss of her head, and her hands on her hips, she had to wait for a truck. She would be charming like that before the minister if she was forced to go that far. Bailey caught a scent of Georgie's perfume and in a rush of love she wished that Tom could have heard how she talked about the Peabodys. A bottle of Peabody gin! God, he would be so happy to hear that!

"Costume." Bailey read the letters on the door that Georgie had opened and then watched patiently for her mother to come back out to the shop.

'What's the costume for, ma?" Bailey reached over the seat and rapped the large box.

"I went to the liquor store."

"C-O-S-T-U-M-E," Bailey carefully spelled. "Does that spell liquor?"

Georgie rolled down the window and furiously waved on the line of cars.

"Come on, come on – dummies. Let me in. You won't? YOU WON'T?"

Bailey hid her face as Georgie charged the traffic.

"Oh, she angry ..." Georgie grinned at the blast of horns and looked into the mirror. Her groceries had spilled on the floor and now she was holding up the entire city while she picked them up. "Have some manners next time," Georgie yelled at the mirror. "Yes, you!"

The large package that her mother had tossed onto the back seat was also on the floor with the top thrown off. Bailey saw a navy blue jacket with gold epaulets and buttons. Her mouth dropped open for the obvious question, when Georgie tapped her on the knee and cordially said, "Absolutely, that spells liquor, my darling little spy. And the reason that box is so large is that when Jack Bailey comes home from the war, there's gonna be booze! Lots and lots of booze!"

Chapter 14

It was still raining in the late afternoon and almost dark. Bailey kept her back straight as she sat at the kitchen table and drank her tea. Since early morning, she'd stood straight, sat straight, walked straight, for in expectation of her father's homecoming she was wearing her navy uniform. Last night she'd forgotten to lock the bathroom door and Georgie had barged into her nightly game. Having just flown her twenty-seventh mission she was perched on the toilet top opposite the mirror, and was answering the many questions of her debriefing when Georgie discovered her.

So braced for mockery, it took Bailey several moments to realize that the small space was awash with compliments. The military style became her tremendously. How distinguished she looked, how handsome! Soft, denying words streamed from her mouth, but as Georgie corroborated her own opinion that the uniform vastly improved her appearance, she finally agreed that she would celebrate her father's arrival by looking as "Navy" as he.

"Damn you, rain," Bailey said aloud when she woke the next morning and snapped up the shade. Today of all days, bright sun and sky should do the honors, but the house, thanks to Cary, was wonderfully clean. To keep her uniform as crisp as possible, Bailey picked up her room and made her bed before she put it on. It was a risk to eat breakfast in it, but as her father could appear at any time during the day it was the only safe thing to do.

Her nerve failed as Georgie's sour eyes lifted from the newspaper and watched her take her place at the table. Pushing back her chair, she was about to make a dash for the kitchen when she saw that Tom and Cary approved of the uniform and silently welcomed her into their ecstatic mood. Patrolling the front windows, back and forth, as the rain fell throughout the day, Bailey felt her nobility and goodness as physically as the weight of her military jacket.

While Bailey finished her tea, the window that looked out on the driveway looked like a mirror hung on the stormy night. The wind was harsh in the trees and against the house. Her small size in the reflecting window did not diminish her narcissism and she seriously stared. In the small kitchen scene on the windowpane the back door swung open.

Bailey saw her military figure shoot to its feet, and there behind her was bent head of a man in a soaked fedora. For the minuscule doings in the window, the suitcase shooting over the threshold, the man's breathing was as loud as the wind. He straightened as Bailey finally looked directly at the open door and bowed his head with a kind smile.

No one but her father could take off his hat with that air of stately care; and how many other men unbuttoned their overcoats from the middle with one hand working up and the other down?

"Dad?" She recognized his hands and his features but her impression of standing in front of a stranger did not abate.

"Why are you sitting in the kitchen?" He frowned up at the flickering ceiling light. "That bulb's about to go. Is the ladder still behind the cellar door? Let me clear the deck here." He carefully put his hat on the table then slowly pushed the suitcase past the cellar door.

"You look so different," said Bailey, helping him with the ladder.

"You too." He put his foot on the first rung. "Taller. Prettier. Get a grip on yourself, Jack. The ladder's steady. You've never fallen before. Nuts!" His foot went back to the floor. "Hey, Navy! Nothing frightens you. Get on up there and change that bulb."

Bailey climbed the ladder, exchanged the burnt-out bulb for the one her father handed up, and she jumped down.

"Dad you can't be afraid of heights, you fly planes."

"Fly planes?" Jack Bailey made a comic face. "Where'd you get that?"

Her father's eyes had always been so hard and quick, the result, Bailey thought, of his manager's job, all that checking and fixing. In front of him, she'd always ranked herself as one of the many objects that he was not so much to see but to keep in line. Now, his bright, still eyes were fixed on her. A look of mild bewilderment kept tugging up his brows.

"You look so different, Dad."

"I feel different, I can tell you."

Lifting his suitcase, he breathed hard again and Bailey ran to hold open the pantry door. As he looked up at the water stain on the dining-room ceiling, his head tilting slowly right and left, she braced for his temper.

"I see a face in that water spot. I see a poor, sad bastard. Do you?"

"Here comes Tom," Bailey said as her father stepped into the hall. He dropped the suitcase and cowered back as Tom jumped off the landing with a yell of delight. Tom's passionate hug, his kisses, could have been a torrent of freezing water as Jack Bailey winced and threw up his arms.

"I'm a wreck," he laughed. Falling back on the couch, he pulled up his pant leg and showed a short cast. "The other day I was walking along the hall to lunch and a small bone in my ankle just up and cracked. Can you beat it?" He smiled placidly up at Tom. "I injured my ankle just walking to lunch. Well, how are you?"

Bailey shared Tom's amazement. Their father was vigorous and bold. What was he doing with stooped shoulders and this frail formality? When Cary plunged screaming down the stairs, he held her off while she danced in front of him and extended his cheek for her to kiss. "Easy now," he murmured. "Go easy."

Tom and Cary had talked at great length about what they would wear to greet their father. They'd spent the weekend shopping and had ended up with a green wool dress for Georgie and two dark brown suits. Following her father's wondering gaze from Tom to Cary, she worshipped their handsome, dark looks.

"By god, you're all in uniform," he tugged Bailey's navy skirt. "The house is as tidy as a barracks. It was all slapdash and spotty when I left. Tom's wild hair, your gypsy clothes, Bailey playing catch in the hall …"

He winked at Cary. "What's happened?"

"We thought you shouldn't be the only one." Cary looked nervously at Tom.

"Where's your uniform, Dad?"

"My uniform?" Jack Bailey waved Tom back and tipped over his suitcase. He sat on the couch and opened it with vague hands.

"Did your mother talk about uniforms? Uniforms, window bars, all that sort of thing? Ah, she's a romantic. I bet she looks the same. Wild hair, wild clothes and spots. Here it is, Bailey. I made it in shop."

Bailey put down the box beside him on the couch and tugged off the cover.

"Pick it up. It's light as a feather."

Tom crowded her as she lifted a wooden plane from the box. It was painted blue with 'Bailey' painted in white letters down the sides.

Tom stroked the wing. "You made a glider, Dad?"

"It's a corker." Her father's amused, quiet gaze turned Bailey into a rock. "It flies like a dream. I must have built a dozen before I got it right, but I sure wasn't going to come home empty-handed for your birthday."

Pushing back Tom's eager hands, Bailey looked into her father's serene face. If intelligence were a form and not a process, it would be her father's eyes and cheekbones. It would be his mouth, his nose and forehead. Until this moment she'd admired his beauty in glances and from afar. She'd never smelled his body or felt the warmth of his flesh and never had she put a name to the color of his eyes. Green! His eyes were green!

"Turning from Tom's reaching hand, she saw Cary disapproving.

"Dad remembered your birthday, Bailey. Say something."

"No," she murmured as Tom asked to hold the glider. She ran up the stairs and locked the door behind her. She put the glider on the dresser then hung onto the corners as she cried. She despised this sudden sorrow, which she could neither control nor understand, and she mocked her face growing red and swollen in the mirror. Tom pounded up the stairs calling for Georgie. She heard Cary's quick step then her father, his hand creaking the banister in the new timidity of his body.

Although in the gentlest way, her father had mocked the military quality of the house and the appearance of the three of them. She'd mooned so over her new appearance. Hour upon hour in front of the bathroom mirror, her eyes had cruised her spruce dark form and the gold anchors on her blue lapel. As her father reached the top of the stairs, Bailey plunged her hands between the gold buttons and opened the jacket from the top and bottom. She tore at the waist, the button flying as the skirt dropped onto her feet then she opened the closet door and gave it a disgusted kick.

"Ma!" Like a huge, green cushion, Georgie lay inside her closet among the clothes.

"Where is he?" Georgie slipped her hands under the straps of Bailey's undershirt and allowed herself to be pulled from the closet. "This green thing makes me look so fat. I look dreadful. Oh, Jesus!" Georgie panicked at the voices outside the door and dragged Bailey back into the closet. "Shut the door," she pleaded. "Please, please shut it!"

Bailey was struggling to get her back instead of her chest against her mother's thick body, when Georgie reached over her shoulder and pulled shut the door. She soon ached in her clench of modesty. Her shoulders held Georgie's elbows and her head heated up with the weight of her chin. The sounds of her mother's insides were so loud – liquid rushing, ticks, twangs and rumblings – that Georgie's whispered monologue was only clear in little bits.

She was bad, so bad to hide this way, but a year was so long! Jack was a stranger to her now. She was afraid of him. She didn't want the drinking, dreaded the fighting. She hated and feared the sex!

"I'm afraid, Bailey!"

Like mud, Bailey had always dreaded her mother's body. Sucky stink and strangulation was the presumed fate of a prolonged embrace, but oddly (was it the thick wool material?) Bailey found she could have been lying on an air mattress for the neutrality of contact. She put her arms around Georgie's waist and lifted her face.

"He's so changed! He's shrunk and very quiet. He looks so puzzled at everything. He made me a glider for my birthday."

Georgie turned the handle and butted out of the closet. Bailey hopped on her trampled feet, softly moaning.

"When was your birthday? Not yet," Georgie accused her. "I don't forget birthdays. November the 21st, am I right? Absolutely! I don't forget birthdays. What? Oh, shit!

The 23rd? Balls, it's December! Is it a state secret, your birthday? Couldn't you have let me know? I've been so upset since your father waltzed out of here. I'm not used to living without a man. The bills! The taxes! The guilt! You rob me blind and spend the year at the movies. It's too hard for Tom to drink, smoke and play sports, so obviously he clears the deck for decadence. And look what Cary does to me the minute I'm all alone? She surrenders to your father's genes. Her sainted Pa is gone two months and I've got an Irish peasant on my hands – as Irish as Paddy's pig. Long centuries of maudlin martyrdom reenacted for my lonely witness, and now you condemn me for forgetting your birthday. What? You laugh at me, you brutal girl!"

"T.V. comics stink compared to you, Ma." Bailey went to the door and unlocked it. "He's looking for you. He'll be so hurt."

Georgie looked down at her dress then stared at Bailey, pale with fear. "I'm enormously green."

"It's cocktail time, Ma." Planting Georgie at the top of the stairs, she put her hand on the banister and nudged her back. "Dad's making you a drink, just like always. Go down, please, he'll be so glad to see you."

When Georgie reached the bottom of the stairs and started towards the library, Bailey's heart began to beat as though she were running. The library, where her parents would finally come together, was beneath her room and the floor which she crossed to get her socks and sneakers felt thin as Kleenex in her extreme aversion. According to her heart and lungs she was already in flight, but not out into the night with its rain and moaning wind. Upstairs then. Upstairs to Cary. Cary who might talk to her. Who always let her sit for a while at the bottom of her bed.

"But that was in another country and besides, the wench is dead." Bailey went cautiously from Cary's doorway to the small room on the other side of the hall. Her father was sitting at a small wooden desk and holding up a book to the dim desk lamp. "But that was in another country." He crossed his legs and smiled kindly at her.

"I always thought that was Shylock's line. It sounds like Shakespeare, don't you think? Do I really think that or did I just forget Christopher Marlowe? It's been twenty-five years since I've read either, and Bailey," he closed the book and faced her with his hands clasping his knee, "I forgot about this room. Now that you're back in civilian dress, I want very much to confide in you. I don't recall ever seeing this room before."

It was a small, white room. A dormer window divided the steeply pitched ceiling into irregular sections. A shabby green easy chair was tucked up against the window. A white bookcase stood against the one flat wall and a red cotton rug covered the floor. Besides the easy chair and the desk, the only other furniture was a small wooden chair that her father was sitting on.

"This was mother's study." Bailey pointed to the jammed bookcase. "Those are her books."

"Your mother hasn't read a book in years and this place is clean as a whistle."

"Cary cleans it every week. Tom and Cary say that before her father died, mother was working for her degree."

Startled, Jack Bailey went over to the bookcase. He

bent to see the lower shelves, his hands on his knees.

"It's all Hegel." He straightened up with an amazed smile. "Georgie was interested in Hegel? Was she actually working for her degree?" Dropping down on the green chair, he crossed his legs and rubbed his fine, gray hair into youthful swirls.

"I was going to read the Harvard Classics," he pointed at the floor. "You know, those two shelves of red books down in the library. Did I ever tell you that it was athletics that got me through college? I never got educated because of athletics! I remember what a brain your mother was – a good teacher, too. The first year we were married I read all the way to 'E'. Five volumes of great thinkers. I remember liking Darwin. I was quite surprised at my interest. At college I had to cheat to get the work done, I'm such a slow reader." Bailey felt so easy in the focus of his still, bright eyes.

"I had a hell of a time doing the work. I didn't do it," he cheerfully laughed. "Albie Taylor got me through. Albie Taylor and classic comics. You look as though you burn the print off the page. You can thank Georgie for that."

He was talking over her tiny voice as he rambled on. "In the old days she was the most intelligent – what?" He uncrossed his legs and leaned forward. "Did you say that you couldn't even read your own name?"

"Don't you remember?" As Bailey described racing to the library from all points of the house to stand at attention before him, he shook his head, smiling, as if she were telling him a joke.

"I forced you to read aloud?"

"Remember when I was reading about that London prison and I couldn't read my name? I thought you'd never stop calling me 'Old Bailey'."

Bailey raised her eyebrows in imitation of his wide, questioning gaze. A look of dread passed quickly over his face then he caught her hand in a hard grip.

"I remember, I remember," he said quickly.

When he pulled her gently to the chair and put his arm around her waist, Georgie's dreadful accusations against him made Bailey struggle away. She dreaded his lower body as she dreaded the powerful black dog when she rode her bike to town. When her parents fought, Georgie would seek refuge behind Bailey's locked door. Sitting in the dark on Bailey's bed, she would describe her ordeal while Bailey grew cold at the thought of the monster that her father became. Her mind refused to give a form to his savage penis, but her stomach, after Georgie crept away, ached from its imagined force.

Expecting an insult, Bailey backed up to the door. Her father's snarl was no less frightening than the neighbor's black dog and Bailey was set to fly.

"Same old nut," he wistfully smiled. "Same old Bailey."

"I'm contagious, Dad. My temperature is one hundred and two."

"Are you missing school?"

In the days before he'd gone off to war, the consequence of missing even an hour of education was so evident in his stern breakfast gaze, that all day long, safe in the peaceful house, worry nibbled at the edges of her pleasure. Now, in all his moods, mildness appeared to replace his terrific intensity. When she told him that Dr. Peabody had ordered her to bed for two weeks, he nodded thoughtfully and in the calmest, friendliest way, told her that he'd been a terrible reader.

"You know, I didn't read a book until the eighth grade – I couldn't."

"You couldn't?"

He'd taken to writing his parents while he was away. One of the letters he'd received from his mother had rocked him off his pins. She'd reminded him of vacations and the summers they'd struggled together to teach him how to read. His answering letter had furiously berated her. She must be senile if she thought that he'd been unable to read. He just hadn't wanted to. He'd been lazy, not stupid.

"Well, she laid it all out. She described the table where we used to work, the dictionary and the magnifying glass that she had to use to look up words. On those long, hot summer days, she thought I'd push her out of the way. I was so desperate to be outside. I wanted to be a gardener like my Dad, but she'd have none of that. It was my sacred duty to learn the vowels. Those vowels!"

He pressed his temples in comic desperation. "Long and short, hard, soft and silent. Unbearable, eh, Bailey?"

She lightly tapped her head against the wall. "No way!"

He held out his hands then quickly clamped them behind his back. His gaze was pleasant and respectful. "I'm going to teach you like my mother taught me, if it takes a month or a year. Time, you know, is a vicious nag, but it doesn't exist with the correct kind of thinking. I'll teach you that too." He stood and made her an elegant bow.

"When I was worked to despair, my mother used to read to me. She'd peer into her magnifying glass and zip along. I'd be happy to read to you, Bailey, any book you like."

"You bet, Dad!" Bailey's flash of sarcasm left her in tears. "Mother promised to teach me the math flash cards but when I bought them at Cameron's and took them to her, she acted like I was fresh. You're the same way."

"Not any more, not any more. You won't believe it until you see it and I don't blame you. Listen, Bailey, I've only been away for three hundred and sixty-five days, but that year seemed longer than the decade that went before. I feel as though I've stepped out of a fog. Over and over again I found myself thinking, 'where the hell have I been?'"

"Ten years is my whole life!" Bailey shouted, amazed at herself. "I don't even have a lousy first name."

Accepting her rage with serene regret, Jack Bailey held out his arms. "Not yet, you fool." He chided himself. "You can pick a damn name from any damn book when you're reading. Tomorrow morning and every morning after that you're going to see that I'm dedicated. You're going to hate my dedication; you're going to hate me."

"All right, no more talk." He held up his hands with a charming smile. "Tomorrow after breakfast, I'm going to hunt you down. Tomorrow morning and every morning. King Lear's speech to Cordelia when they've been captured by the French, his description of how they'll live together in prison is so moving." His hand to his ear, he stole to the head of the stairs. "I believe I hear your mother, Bailey. We'd best go down."

He was so different. He earnestly watched the stairs and a few, faint clinks of the change in his pockets accompanied his careful descent. Before, the loud jolt of coins as he flew up and down, could be heard all over the house. Bailey held the third-floor door for him then followed across the upstairs hall and on the next flight of stairs, she frowned as he did and watched her timid feet. She heard the kitchen door swing open and smelled the food that Cary was cooking for Jack's first night home. Roast beef, she'd insisted, was his favorite meal. Georgie had wanted shad. Cary was bringing in cheese and crackers.

When she looked towards the stairs and saw her father, she joyfully shouted for Georgie, then nipped into the library, scattering crackers on the rug. As Tom and Cary excitedly ordered Georgie into the hall, Jack Bailey sank down on the stairs. He put his elbows on his knees and, softly whistling, held his head.

Similar in height and hair, equally serious in their new brown suits, Tom and Cary looked like Georgie's official escort. Each holding an arm, they brought her up to the stairs and stepped back.

Leaning forward, Jack Bailey peered at her new green shoes and tapped them, one after the other. Georgie's greeting gesture was so muffled with shyness that Bailey wanted to grab that drifting hand and plant it on her father's shoulder. She took a step back as Jack Bailey reached for the banister and pulled himself up.

"Hello," she croaked. "I'm fat and much too green." Her feet dragged as he tugged her against him. As their cheeks met and his hands pulled at her waist, Georgie arched her back and Bailey, terribly squeamish, noted the generous space between their lower bodies.

"Dad's home!" Tom cheered. "Good, old Dad!"

In the dining room, Bailey went around the table and lit the tall silver candle sticks. Jack Bailey seated Georgie, and Bailey could feel his eyes on her back as he walked to his old place opposite her mother. Her breath held, her clenched stomach began to ache as she waited for his criticism. His expression was affectionate when she looked round. Pleasure flooded her, then anxiety and resentment that this wonderful new mood of his would probably be gone in the morning.

She lit the candelabra on the sideboard and could feel Tom's happiness as he carved the roast beef. With a compliment and a tap on the shoulder, Jack Bailey had bequeathed the carving job to Tom and had gone into the kitchen to look for more soda. Before dinner, he'd fixed three drinks for Georgie but over the ice cubes in his own glass he'd poured soda water.

While Tom seriously carved and Cary served the plates, Jack Bailey said how glad he was to be sitting once again in this charming room. There hadn't been a night, the year he was away, that he hadn't mentally followed the route of his bedtime check. In his mind he'd never failed to try the doors, turn down the furnace and turn off the lights.

"I began to appreciate this lovely little place." He turned his serene gaze from Georgie's scowl and smiled at Bailey who was sitting on his right. "The rooms are small but elegant. I'd doze off thinking about the old floors and the moldings. I'd imagine the rooms when you were all asleep. What a wonderful old guardian, I'd think, as I heard the furnace humming in my mind, I'd hear all the creaks and groans of the old walls. On moonlit nights the windows formed such sweet squares of light. When it snowed I'd imagine the slate roof slowly covering and the evergreen dropping as the storm went on."

Georgie pointed up at the wet spot on the ceiling behind him. "Odd you didn't imagine the rain seeping into Cary's ceiling through the leaky roof, or the stopped-up toilets or the dead light sockets." Her mean, pale eyes blinked continuously. "Perhaps that's why the rain has been so destructive. It was excluded from your benevolent mind." She raised her wine glass. "Do you think?"

Jack Bailey drank from his water glass. "I also used to think about our well, how deep it was and what sort of earth the water passed through to be so good. If you ever move away, Bailey, you'll learn how lucky you've been all your life – water-wise." He rolled his eyes like a shy comedian.

Cary put down Tom's plate then served herself. They sat down at the same time. Even more than their similar looks and clothes, the intense, expectant expression that they shared made them look like twins.

Jack Bailey poured gravy on his beef. As he ate, his face grew rosy with pleasure. "It's superb," he sighed. His absorption in the food suggested the bleakness of his wartime diet and made his children feel guilty and shy. Wiping his brow, he looked around the table at their half-filled plates.

"I can't remember ever having beef as good as this. The gravy is excellent, Cary. Eat, all of you. Eat, Georgie."

Putting down her wine glass, Georgie gave her plate a rude little shove. "I'm too disappointed to eat. I expected to see a god walk up the front walk. The epaulets, the medals, the gold buttons! You're a mere mortal." She softly belched. "I could cry."

Jack Bailey yanked loose his tie as he looked round at the four of them and unbuttoned the top of his shirt. The old chair squealed with his uneasy movement.

"Don't you remember that I asked you to think about wearing a uniform so that the children could see what you looked like?"

"But you assumed that I would." He glanced at Tom. "Why did you tell the children that I'd wear my uniform home? I didn't have time to answer your letter."

Georgie drank off a glass of wine. "It was such a terrific idea! I thought you'd see that. I don't see why you didn't – for the children."

"That's all right, Dad." Tom was upset. "You couldn't wear your pilot's uniform home and that's the one I wanted to see. Who cares about your dress uniform, right, Cary?"

An invisible force seemed to be hurling Jack Bailey from the table. His eyes sought Georgie's while his hands clutched the arms of his chair. "The so-called Navy wouldn't let me fly planes. With my eyes and reflexes? Even if I had qualified as a pilot I'd have spent most of my year in the hospital. Surely, your mother told you I had hemorrhoids? You knew that, didn't you, Tommy?"

Tom swayed in his chair, chewing his lips to bits.

Georgie laughed and hurried to drink her wine. Her gulping and the gurgling in her throat were crudely loud. "You don't have to tell the kids in school about the hemorrhoids, Tommy." She sighed and licked her lips. "He's bragged about you, Jack. He's so proud of his patriotic father."

Tom could hardly breathe. "I don't boast, Dad."

Georgie put down her glass with a malicious smile. "You've boasted, all right. We all have. What's the to-do? I exaggerate, I get carried away! It's my nature."

"You're so proud of your nature – that's what I can't stand." Tom's face was crimson and the vein in his neck stood out, rapping with blood.

Georgie poured wine in her glass with a gleaming smile. Insult invigorated her and pumped up her girth to a thick imperviousness.

She's a bullfrog, Bailey thought as Georgie lifted the overflowing glass to her lips, but she sure ain't gonna sing.

As Georgie wheezed and gulped, Jack Bailey got up and took the roast beef platter out to the kitchen. Looking grim and haggard, Tom piled up all the plates and banged through the kitchen door. Glasses clinked in Cary's careful hands and Bailey grabbed the napkins.

"Hey," she cried as Georgie reached out and pulled her against her side.

"Hey, yourself. Hey, hey, hey. I'm in the doghouse, ain't I?" She gazed ruefully at Bailey, her body a swamp of sounds. "I did exaggerate. Damn it, I always do and I forgot your birthday. Will you ever forgive me?"

Bailey kissed her doleful cheek. "I was never mad at you." Looking into her mother's commanding eyes, she

96

obediently read a script. She knew how sad Georgie was, and she knew why she was sorry for her – it was awful about her father. Georgie straightened and energy welled in her eyes. Bailey read rapidly on. What was a forgotten birthday compared to her mother's grief? Until her own father died, she could only guess at her mother's pain, but certainly, she would never add to it.

"He does, though." Georgie murmured.

"You're funny, Ma!" Bailey pulled gently away. "You're funny and nice. You're also smart."

Georgie nodded in vigorous agreement. "That was a smart idea. It was a terrific idea! I'm smart!" Bailey lunged to catch the falling chair as Georgie stood. "I'm bright as two pennies." Bailey heard her mother panting up the stairs. I am very smart," she shouted.

Jack Bailey crouched by the kitchen sink. Suds floated from his hand as he swung through a forehand drive. He smiled at Tom. "Georgie tells me you've got some good strokes. I bet you have."

Bending his knees, Tom pranced back. "Forehand, backhand, overhead." Bailey avoided his powerful arm. "My serve's the best. I guess that's the easiest to practice."

"Your mother's a good teacher."

"I got it from the pros on T.V." Tom stopped dead in a black mood. As his father checked the kitchen shelves and stooped to look under the sink, a cruel smile flickered on Tom's mouth. The sharp crack of Jack Bailey's knees as he pulled himself up, turned his anger to pity and he glared at Bailey for watching him.

The kitchen door crashed against Bailey's back. She

leapt for the top of the dishwasher as the heavy door sailed inward.

"Attention!" Bailey saw a small, blue form reflected on the kitchen window. Cary's shock as she turned from the sink was frightening and she drew her legs up on the warm top of the dishwasher. Jack Bailey seemed to shrivel still smaller. He glanced at Tom then stole to the other end of the kitchen.

Georgie greeted them with a pugnacious smile. An officer's cap covered half her face and she appeared to be saluting with a stump as the gold-striped cuff flapped down. Her pant legs bunched on the linoleum floor.

Jack Bailey came up to the kitchen table and leaned on a chair. "You absurd woman. What for?"

"To show the kids." A panel of medals heaved on Georgie's excited breast. "If you won't, then I will. You're too old to be a patriot. You could have ignored the war, like all the men of your generation, but you are a patriot, so you hammered the Navy into taking you. The kids should appreciate that. They should know what a god you looked like."

Absurdly pompous, Georgie glared at her three children. Their disgust frightened her and she stepped back against the door. "No!" she rallied herself. Tipping back the cap, she insolently smiled and thumbed her nose. "You can see what I've been through." She winked at her husband and threw herself into his arms. Tugging his ears, rumpling his hair, she pushed her face against his with an excited laugh.

"No, Georgie." He turned his mouth from her lips and pushed her back. "It's distasteful to the children."

Chapter 15

"The way we split." In Cary's room, at the top of the house, Tom sorted through a pile of records with a nervous laugh. "It was a cartoon. Va-voom! The three of us all hit the door together."

Tom and Bailey had hauled their sleeping bags from the trunk in the attic and spread them on the floor by Cary's bed, as was their custom when their parents fought. Who would have thought that their custom would be so quickly renewed?

Tom put Tchaikovsky on the stereo. "Good," he murmured as the symphony began. "Kettledrums, trumpets cymbals and cannon, even Ma can't howl over that."

Cary sat at her dressing table, rolling up her hair. While Tom and Bailey dug out the sleeping bags, she'd changed into her nightgown. She criticized Tom for mucking about in his new suit and told him to go downstairs to change.

"No way! I'm out of condition for their brawls. I'm staying right here."

Tom turned down the volume and they listened for the sounds of their parents' rampage – the horrid thudding and the hoarse panting of Georgie's pain.

"It's so quiet." Shivering, Tom wrapped himself up in his sleeping bag.

"Dad looks so different. Those big, questioning eyes. At first I thought he was on drugs, but his eyes are too clear. He's not drinking." He sought Cary's eyes in the heart-shaped mirror. "At least not tonight. When he's passed up drinks before, Mother's always blasted him – not a word from her. It's so fucking strange."

"Not really." Cary stared at her image with her usual satisfaction. "I don't think he's had much to drink since he's been away. After all," she fingered a piece of hair, "he's been in training."

Tom watched the mirror with ironic expectation. He gave Bailey one of his wacky, incredulous looks and asked Cary whether she didn't think it strange that despite the naval training, in his own words, Jack Bailey looked a wreck.

"He was too old to go, Tom. What would build you up, just wore him down." Cary sprayed her neck with perfume and turned round with a comforting smile. "That's also the reason why he got those –"

"Hemorrhoids," Tom finished with a sad laugh.

"If you're going to be so disgusting, you can just get out."

Her priggishness enraged him. He confronted her anger with a supercilious sneer and was about to attack when a door slammed on the second floor. In a second his fury turned to dread. He could not bear to be kicked out of Cary's room tonight.

"I'll jump out the window," he whispered, "if Mother comes up here. Whenever she brought up his uniform, he looked so, so … "

"Guilty?" Cary frowned.

"Exactly. Dad looked as though he wanted to crawl out of his skin and she saw that, she enjoyed that. Horrible!" Tom shivered.

"She looked so pathetic in the kitchen when no one would look at her." Bailey was miserable. "She was like a kid when Dad wouldn't get into this costume. Don't you spell costume, c-o-s-t-u-m-e?"

So intent to tell her story well, to not bore Tom and Cary with unnecessary details or annoy them with the mispronunciation of words, Bailey didn't take in their fear and alarm as she told them about the costume shop and the box banging open to show a navy uniform and Georgie's cheerful lie about buying booze for their father's homecoming. Their cold disapproval as she finished completely confused her.

When Cary got up from her dressing table and turned down her bed, when Tom turned off the stereo, shut it up and then walked past her to switch on the TV, she felt their movement erasing her.

It was like a dream where the mysterious is instantly accepted but unlike in a dream where the emotion is named but not felt, she suffered the panic of their inexplicable reaction. Between their remote bodies, on the floor, she felt so suddenly repugnant to them that she dared not make the slightest movement. To get up and scurry from the room was too brutal an exposure, so she cringed down in the sleeping bag and silently breathed.

Tom scouted to the bottom of the stairs and announced that the house was quiet. If Cary would like, he'd sneak down to the kitchen and make some cocoa. When Tom had gone, Cary adjusted the image on the T.V. screen then got to her feet with a groan. The frank sound was startling and Bailey, lying flatter in the sleeping bag, realized that Cary had forgotten that she was in the room. Her tense whispering made Bailey's throat ache.

"Oh, God, I love him so much! Please God, you've got to help me. You've got to make Jim call. I'm not bad. I'm like all the girls I know. I'm not bad! Make Jim love me! Make him marry me! Please, please, PLEASE!"

When Cary went into the bathroom and closed the door, Bailey made a dash down the stairs. Georgie stood in the hall and rattled the knob of the guest room door. She swayed and hissed through the wood. Her nightgown had fallen off her shoulders and her fat breasts were slung down her chest.

"This bastard," she informed Bailey. "This ball-less bastard has locked himself in. I want a drink! Will you, my darling Bailey, get me a drink?"

"If you go back to bed."

"I will," Georgie said obediently. "I'll go to bed this instant."

When Bailey came back upstairs with the drink, Georgie was back at the guest room door. "It's my money. My house," she hissed and rattled the doorknob. Her forehead cracked against the wood.

"Come on, ma." The ice tinkled gaily in the glass of scotch as Georgie followed her drink through the hall and into her bedroom. She settled docilely in bed and held out her hand for the drink.

"Women don't like to be raped, I told him. I was bad, Bailey, his first night back, but I wasn't ready for him – I never am – and the pain made me blurt it out. I'm so terrible to have said that on his first night home." The liquor passed down her throat in loud remorse.

Every time Georgie took a swallow, Bailey guided the glass back to the antique table that stood between the beds. It was covered with rings from the years of Georgie's nightcaps and Bailey always landed the glass on one of the existing circles.

"You're not bad, Ma." While her crossed arms guarded her chest, her legs were the lock to the lower half of her body and they ached as she pressed them together.

"I'm not bad!" Georgie's stout nods pumped Bailey's head. "I was just so upset by what he told me. Do you know what he told me? Your father wants to quit working for the club. He wants to go back to Bailey Street."

"Terrific!" Bailey clapped her hands. "Tom will be so happy."

Bailey laughed at Georgie's great droop of astonishment, her incredulous eyes. "Bailey Street? Those awful, little houses? Those vulgar people? Live there? What?"

"Grandma and Grandpa Bailey have a nice house, Ma."

"That stuffy little parlor with the rose wallpaper – those lace curtains? The furniture shining like the moon, those little lace doilies like flattened starfish everywhere under your hands. Little lace doilies on the slipcovers?" Georgie's eyes lifted past Bailey's and beheld the grotesque above her head. "Jesus is nailed up everywhere. Rosy lips and sweetheart curls. A big, round valentine heart shines through his robe and he smiles like this."

Bailey shouted with laughter at the slippery, sweet smile of Georgie's lips. "That's just the way they live."

"What?" The heavy glass slipped slowly through her fingers. Bailey lunged and nipped the gold rim of the glass in her fingers.

"Athlete." Georgie sank down in bed. Her foot poked from beneath the covers and hung over the rug. "An athlete, a philosopher. My girl Bailey. Best of the litter. Your father looks like a philosopher with his beseeching eyes but apparently he's just gone mad. Back to Bailey Street after all these years? He'd hate it more than any of us. What do you think has changed him so?"

"Stockbridge, maybe?" As Bailey pushed Georgie's foot under the sheet and tightened the bedclothes in a sturdy hospital corner she felt suddenly clumsy. Looking up, she was startled by Georgie's alarm.

"Do you feel sick?" She thought of what she could bring if Georgie should vomit.

"He told you. I can't believe he'd tell you. Why didn't he let me know?"

This timidity was as amazing to Bailey as her mother's faulty memory. Georgie was never really drunk until six and so surely she could not have forgotten that when she and Dr. Peabody were talking about Stockbridge, Bailey had been putting on her clothes in the office next door.

"I heard it with the stethoscope." As she again explained how she'd played around with the stethoscope, how she'd sounded the wall in imitation of Dr. Peabody's examination of her chest, Georgie's seriousness seemed too heavy for the prank.

"He told you! I can't believe he told you," Georgie repeated when Bailey stopped talking. She was furious. "When did he tell you? Exactly what did he say?"

"I just heard him say Stockbridge — maybe three times." Bailey grinned. "I heard it with my little stethoscope."

The word "stethoscope" was like a fly on the thick hide of Georgie's mind. Landing, twitched off, her consciousness was filled with something else.

"He's going to pay for that. I did my half. I worked like a dog to do my half." Georgie's growing malice was terrifying, "I suppose you told Tom and Cary?"

Bailey jumped over the bed and hugged Georgie from behind as she stood up.

"I get the costume. I'm in the kitchen trying to make it all happen. I'm drowning in that damn uniform and all the time you kids know. GODDAMN!"

Bailey jumped on her mother's back as she went into the hall. From Georgie's total indifference to her weight, Bailey knew that she was just another fly on the surface of her mind. That impression was awful and Bailey realized that it would grow worse when she was alone. Much of the night was still ahead and even though she knew her clinging and pleading would make Georgie violent, Bailey wrestled off the moment of separation with all her strength. Every time Georgie would unpeel an arm, a leg would take its place. With Bailey clinging to her neck, Georgie cried that she was choking and she sank down on her knees. In a flash, Bailey had her round the waist, lying on her broad back as she coughed and wheezed.

"Horrible little girl!" Georgie pinched her hands with her strong nails. "Just couldn't wait – oh, she couldn't run fast enough to say mummy is a liar. Stockbridge didn't have to exist, and now Tom hates me because of you." Georgie dug in her nails. "Because of damn little, dumb little you."

"Stockbridge!" Bailey shrieked, and slid off Georgie's back. She sat on her heels, clutching her scratched and punctured hands. "What is it?"

Georgie's spite made her forget her pain. "Oh, now she's playing the little innocent. You're some actress, Bailey, with your dismay and your instant tears and your incredible self pity."

"I don't pity myself! That's what you do. All the time." Up on her heels, her hands holding each other like battered friends, Bailey looked into the stream of Georgie's malice and saw it falter and drop. She saw Georgie flee to her bedroom.

"I hate a brat," she cried and slammed the door.

"I will hate you!" Bailey quietly vowed. In a flash of insight that she hardly remembered when a minute had passed, she realized that her frantic struggle to win Georgie's love was not futile, that her struggle, one far, future day, would free her. Not shivering in the cold of Georgie's selfishness, no longer lamenting, one day, she would hate her joyfully and tenderly, with the deepest good humor.

Chapter 16

"Shut up, cat cunt! Listen to her Bailey, like the cat I used to put in the sink and hold under the cold water when she was in heat. I should go down there with the hose. Spray the fire hole! Oh, she's on her way. Shriek it out, Mother. Let the whole world know. Such a gross jerk! How can Dad get it up?"

"He doesn't dare not to."

Tom jerked round from the door. Bailey's quiet sophistication amazed him and he drowned with embarrassment and guilt.

"You sound like a woman of the world."

"I'm not!" Since she'd come down with her mysterious fever two weeks before Christmas, Bailey had been doing her schoolwork in this attic room that their father had annexed for his use. Tonight she was taking old photographs from a box she'd found in the attic and was pasting them onto the blank pages of a large album. She'd settled in on the floor and when Jack Bailey was not servicing the great beast but was reading in the green easy chair with his feet up on the radiator, the two of them took up all the space that there was.

When Tom came up to visit Cary, the mellow tone of his father reading aloud to Bailey was the steady background of their evening talk. For three hours every morning, Jack Bailey tutored her, and recently, he had been cautiously pleased at her progress. His theory of Bailey's trouble was simple. She'd been badly broken in. The more he worked with her, the more certain he became that the dread of being stupid was creating her difficulty by itself.

"Is it over?" Bailey asked as she pasted.

"She's bitching. Bitching and whining." Tom punched the door. "Get yourself off, Mother. Sit on a bomb!"

There was a light knock on the door. "Careful now, be careful." Jack Bailey edged into the room. He carried a large tray.

"Clear that desk for me, Tom?" Breathing heavily, he inched past Bailey and settled the tray on the desk. He pulled a handkerchief from his pocket and wiped his forehead.

"I didn't know you were here, Tom. I've only two cups." He touched the silver pot. "Still hot, that's good. I made the cocoa with light cream tonight Bailey. It's excellent." He went to the door. As he pushed it open, Georgie's trills and moans floated up the stairwell.

"I thought you were with Mother." Tom's face grew dark as he blushed. "Aren't you?"

"Are I?" Jack Bailey shrugged with a cordial smile. "Could I be? I'll be right back with your cup."

"No!" Tom tugged him back. "I don't want cocoa."

"Really? It's terribly good. Bailey and I have some every night before we go to bed."

As he carefully filled the cups and chatted about the variety of cocoa mixes that he'd tried, the different blends of milk and cream, Tom kept tossing his head and thrusting up his chin. He punched the door wider as Georgie kept up her loud immodest cries and began to jump up and down.

"Easy now." Jack Bailey frowned as he handed Bailey her cup. "This stuff is hot as hell. No accidents, now. No burns. Careful." He put the cup on the table and slowly lowered himself into the shabby green chair. Crossing his legs, he eased his trousers at the knees and seriously, slowly, took up his cup of cocoa. He swallowed and settled the cup on his knee.

These temperate, civilized motions tortured Tom. He ground his teeth and kicked at the floor with his feet, then looked up guiltily at his father and the dainty cup balanced on his knee. His earnest concentration as he drank and replaced the cup in the saucer made Tom beat his leg and then the door.

"Go easy." Jack Bailey's wide questioning gaze switched with no change from his cocoa to his son.

"What is this, Dad?"

"Dr. Peabody? I assume so, don't you? He and Polly were here for dinner."

Tom threw out his arms in agony. "Dad!"

Jack Bailey finished his cocoa and put the cup on the table. He dug his handkerchief from his back pocket and thoroughly wiped his lips, thoroughly folded the large square of white cotton – Tom's arms swung despondently as he watched – and returned the handkerchief to his back pocket.

"I'm sorry you're ashamed of me. I can see you're

confused and depressed by the change in me. How many times you children must have comforted yourselves with the scene of my homecoming – the suitor slain. Poor Tommy! I'm sorry, I really am. I struggled for years to satisfy your mother, to keep the others off. I struggled, knowing it was hopeless, perhaps because it was hopeless – I don't know – I struggled like a drowning man and when I stopped, when I hit bottom, my energy to win your mother, my frantic jealousy, was all burned up." He pointed at the door.

"They could be lined up round the block, one Peabody after the other and I don't care."

"I don't care either," Bailey cried, flourishing the paste stick. "Screw 'em!"

Tom took a step towards her. "Knock it off!" His finger pointed in fury. "One more curse and I'll belt you."

"That's right." Jack Bailey serenely approved. He winked at Bailey. "Did I used to scare you like that?"

"More." Bailey appeased Tom with a quick smile. "You used to make me wet my pants. 'Attention! Sound it out, Bailey!' It was awful!"

Jack Bailey looked pensively at his daughter. "If that's the cause of your terrific rushing, I'm deeply sorry, but, we're fixing that, you know, little by little. You look so miserable, Tommy."

"Dr. Peabody thinks he's the boss around here."

"Bailey sure told him off." Jack Bailey chuckled. "'My sister's not going to marry your son. He's a bottle of gin.' Didn't Georgie hit the roof – not that you cared."

"I don't mind about Mother – not any more."

Waking up after Georgie's attack, Bailey had been

very surprised to find herself weary but unmistakably calm. Her grief at Georgie's wickedness, her long, denying fight was over and her energy, although much weakened, was returned to her to use for her growth. In three weeks she'd learned all the math facts and was whipping through the workbooks that her father ordered through the school.

Twice now she'd gone into the hospital and submitted to the endless tests that Dr. Peabody ordered. Her blood, hormones, her heart and all the vital processes of her body, were normal and yet, thankfully, her elevated temperature continued. Physically, but for the fever, she was normal and working with her father – "hell no, honey, four times nine is not twenty-seven," his mild, predictable humor checking her despair. She was daily putting more weight on her belief that her mind was normal too.

"What's happened to you, Dad?" The words seemed glued to Tom's dry mouth. Watching him, Bailey kept running her tongue over her lips. "You're such a wimp."

"Wimp?"

"You're not a wimp." Tom thrust out his chin. "I didn't mean it. I really didn't mean it."

"It's painful to think your father's a coward. I'm sorry."

"You weren't a wimp before!" Tom desperately encouraged him. "When you were away, Dr. Peabody was afraid of you. He was always in the house but he never went upstairs. What's happened to you?"

"A religious person would say that he'd been reborn." Jack Bailey smiled at Tom's embarrassment and cleared his throat. "I just woke up. I started to see things. I began to read, even think."

As Bailey imitated her father, her wide, unblinking eyes began to sting. "I slowly came into possession of my memory. Why the hell are people so interested in outer space?" He snapped his fingers in front of his nose. "After forty it's so boring out there."

"Out here, it's humiliating!" Tom thrust his hand to his hair and viciously yanked. "At dinner, did you hear how Dr. Peabody was ordering your children around? Right now, he's with mother in your own bed. Come on! Come on! Fix things up out here before you retreat to your – philosophy."

"If a man can't satisfy his wife, he should step aside."

"Mother has no right to that! We had to take the insult. What could we do?" Tom punched the low ceiling. "But you don't!"

"I don't take it as an insult."

Tom howled.

Jack Bailey turned his placid, bright eyes to the wall as if he were reading a message above Tom's head. "I choose not to be a jealous husband – it's a short life."

"The name of that is cowardice," Tom snarled. "You're afraid of Dr. Peabody."

"Oh, come now." Jack Bailey pleasantly laughed.

"He thinks you're afraid of him."

"I know I'm not."

"God damn this word crap! I don't want to hear any more!"

Looming over his father as he lectured him, then stepping back and pointing with his forefinger, Tom was so much the way Jack Bailey had been before he'd gone off to fight, that Bailey trembled before this magical effect as if she were seeing a ghost.

"You're no match for Dr. Peabody! No way! Out here!" Tom shouted as Jack Bailey ironically tapped his temple. "Out here you're a pitiful bastard who lets his boss sleep with his wife. You're not screwing Dr. Peabody, Dad, and you don't give orders in his house. I couldn't believe tonight. Dr. Peabody not only tells you that Cary is marrying his son, but he gives you a list of guests he wants invited to the engagement party. There you sat as though you were watching a play. You look that way now!" Tom despaired. "I almost panicked tonight when Mother didn't wade in, but I know that after six we've got the Georgie yes-yes-yes doll. First thing tomorrow morning she'll take that list and rip it up."

"But your mother loves a party."

"You said you got your memory back." Tom was suspicious. "Things haven't changed. Every night Georgie agrees with the Peabodys that Cary and Jim are the world's most enchanting couple." Tom picked up an imaginary glass with an asinine smile. "But the next morning, right after breakfast, she calls up old Polly and tells her the wedding's off."

Looking quickly back and forth between Bailey and Tom, Jack Bailey appeared to be after a clue. "But Cary's so in love."

"That hasn't changed either, Dad." Jack Bailey listened to Tom with dread. "Remember when Cary was smart and funny as hell? She used to be so much fun and she read all the time. Now, she doesn't even pick up the newspaper. All

113

my friends were in love with her and remember all those college guys asking her out when she was only fifteen? Every other month she'd decide on a different career – marriage made her puke. She was going to have affairs and be famous. I don't understand it. What's happened to her, Dad?"

"Fear!" whispered Jack Bailey, his face a vivid illustration.

"What's Cary afraid of?"

"Life."

Tom thrust his tongue into the corner of his mouth and nodded ironically. "Since you've come back, Dad, you've been prone to generalization. Even the tone of your voice has a hollow, impersonal sound, like a priest, like a, ha! Like a philosopher."

"I've seen it."

"What?"

"It."

"Holy Shit!" Tom clutched his head. "Holy, holy shit!"

"You're not so far off." Turning his chair, Jack Bailey smiled at Tom. "Cary's change is normal, Tommy. At her age it's depressing to live at home. Her childhood is over and she yearns to be moving on. She didn't like college and here she feels trapped."

"But why didn't she like college? Why?" Tom thought his father a fool. "Cary's a stranger to you. And you're a snob! If she wanted to marry Jim Ordinary, the drunk, you wouldn't allow it."

Jack Bailey accepted Tom's bitter contempt with a peaceful smile. "I stopped drinking, so will Jim Peabody. If he doesn't, if there's a divorce, there'll be a very generous settlement and Cary, if she wants it, will have the benefit of that name. As I see it, Tommy, either way she'll be better off than rotting at home."

"Cary's just like you. She's not interested in herself any more. Don't you remember when she was your golden girl?" Tom shouted into his father's frightened face. "But now with your shitty 'It' you don't care! You're a selfish bastard! Oh, God!" Tom clutched his head. "I don't know what you went through in the war. I shouldn't have said that."

"Never mind." Gravity seemed to pull at Jack Bailey with terrific force. His mouth struggled against the pressure; his breath struggled from his lungs. He hadn't been in the war, but at Stockbridge to stop drinking.

"You weren't in the Navy?"

"That was the story we told you."

Tom slid down the wall and sat, clasping his knees. Jack Bailey cast quick glances at him and slowly, as he spoke, as though Tom's numbing disenchantment was let in at his eyes, he turned wooden and remote.

"I was so shot at the time. I had no will. It made Georgie happy to say I was enlisting. I knew it was wrong, but last Christmas I was much too sick to argue. As I got better and considered you kids – your letters made me so ashamed – but you know, I'd been drunk for ten years and was used to the feeling and frankly, it was hard to think of you two at all. I retreated to my own childhood on Bailey Street."

"Do you two remember going to visit your

grandparents when you were small? We spent every Thanksgiving there until that damn terrier bit Georgie. Of course, she was looking for an excuse to end that tradition and that was it. Do you remember the big hill with the tunnel going through it? The last Thanksgiving, the day was gloomy when we hit the tunnel, but when we came out the other side – the damn thing was half a mile long – the sun was shining."

"Yellow tiles," Bailey said. "The tunnel had yellow tiles."

"That's absolutely right!" Jack Bailey was delighted. "I'm amazed at you, Bailey. You were only five when that silly mutt bit Georgie."

Turning towards her, Jack Bailey hitched up his shoulders as though to block out Tom. Bailey watched his describing hands with intense excitement. The flying yellow tiles, the song of the car's quick passage and, as they shot from the tunnel, the sunny explosion of space, had endured in Bailey's memory as an isolated incident, a revered incident, the day she'd hurtled into fairyland. The sensation of whipping speed, the mystery of the yellow tiles and the sudden propulsion to ecstasy in that beautiful valley, existed in her memory as an isolated loop of recollection, a tunnel to wonder, but unlike that tunnel through the hillside, it came from oblivion and circled back.

She had been five years old. She'd been riding in the Mercury convertible with her mother and father, Tom and Cary. They were driving to Bailey Street to eat a holiday dinner with her grandparents.

As her father described the marshes, the bay and the short, country street where his family lived, the pictures in her mind were so complete that he seemed to be reviving her memory. Yet when he stopped talking her head went as blank as his silence. The bright blue house where her Uncle Eddy lived, the bulldozer, the long, yellow neck of a steam shovel that loomed over his cousin's barn, did not lead her from one to the other. Although the ancient tree that hid her grandfather's house from the road was perfectly familiar – she could see the yellow patches beneath the peeling bark – she didn't know that the color of his childhood home was brown.

Little by little as he talked, her father had hitched around the heavy chair until its thick back was between him and Tom's heavy misery. Bailey was so involved that for a while she wasn't aware enough of her father to be shy. When she began to take him in, she was surprised to be feeling so natural. Joyfully, she realized that he was treating her like a friend and that he also seemed happy, as though such a conversation was rare in his life.

"Time is the great dread of alcoholics, you know. For a decade that liquor in me so dulled its teeth and nails that I only dealt with smooth, large units. My mind would step out among the weeks and months like an actor. Now and again it would be on the stage, but mostly it was gone." His wondering eyes and smile excited Bailey. "God knows where, my dear. You can imagine the horror of Stockbridge, the first days, oh Jesus, those advancing seconds bristly with guilt. My room was on the first floor right above the furnace.

"At first I despaired at the noise, but then I learned. For years, you know, I'd been diving into liquor, and for the first couple of weeks I could hardly wait until bedtime so that I could dive into the furnace sound. I'd lie there and concentrate for dear life on the humming, the groans and clicks until I corked off. One night, flashing up at me, was Dad's old outboard motor that he gave me when I was eight. Yes!" He vigorously nodded as if Bailey could hardly believe such a thing. "The palm of my hand hurt again. I smelled the gas in the tank. I smelled the bay. The knob of the starting cord was split in half and its edge was bruising my skin." Looking into Bailey's eyes, he laughed with delight. "I'd hauled on that broken knob, I'd fished and dug up clams. I'd been out to the deserted duck blind and blown up coffee and flour cans with cherry bombs. I'd lived moments in another time. That seems such a mystery to me." Jack Bailey looked down at his hands with a bemused smile. "Where is that eight-year-old boy who kept gouging his palm with that damned split knob? Certainly not the hell here. Gone without a trace. Is that the mystery? Why make up exotic places? Why fly into the future on spaceships when it's so exciting to be aware of the constant reincarnation?

"Right now – I don't know why – I'm seeing my mother's dressing table. It had a thick glass top, slightly green in color, and beneath the glass she'd put the family snapshots that she liked. I loved to look at them." He smiled at Bailey. "There are snaps of you there, too – up to the age of five. Dad loved taking pictures of his grandchildren."

Bailey's heart thumped with excitement. "Grandpa took pictures of me? When I was a baby?"

"You couldn't have been more than a week old in one shot. Georgie's holding you."

A few days ago, Bailey had followed her father into the attic and poked around while he checked out the damage from the leaky roof. She'd found a box of photographs and had rushed through them while her father grumbled and poked at the attic ceiling.

"Who was the baby in the white tee shirt?" She'd asked, but it was always Tom or Cary, and in a swirl of disappointment, Bailey went back to the box.

Remembering that whenever she'd begged Georgie to show her pictures of herself when she was a baby, she'd always been put off with vague excuses, she concluded that there were no pictures of her at all. Why take snaps of a kid with no first name?

"Dad, I want to go visit Grandma and Grandpa. I want to go back to Bailey Street."

Jack Bailey cocked up a brow at her vehemence. "Surely, you recall how much your mother loves to take that trip?"

"But, she doesn't have to go. Take me and Tom. Oh, please Dad. Can't we go soon? It would be so great!" Bailey felt almost sick from her yearning to see the pictures of herself that Grandma Bailey kept on her dresser table under the green grass. "Let's go tomorrow. At the crack of dawn."

"Don't I hear your mother now?" Jack Bailey put his hand behind his ear with a teasing smile. "Why don't you go down and ask her? Take the cups." He pointed to the cocoa cups as she bounced up. "Might as well."

Careful with the cups, Bailey went slowly down the stairs. The door separating the third floor from the rest of the house stuck at the top and Bailey put down the cups so that she could bear down. Staring at the pretty glass knob, she thought of its image popping up in her mind when she was as old as her father and tried to imagine his excitement.

Dr. Peabody was standing in the doorway of her parents' bedroom. Dressed, except for his jacket, he wore loafers instead of his usual heavy, brown shoes, and a pair of gray slacks that dropped down his long, lean legs without a wrinkle. As he tied his necktie a cruel smile came and went on his lips.

"I made you, Georgie," he crisply broke into her mutterings. "Now you make the bed."

"Get me off, you bastard!"

Bailey froze where she stood.

Her head drooping, Georgie laboriously crawled towards Dr. Peabody. Tucking his thumbs into his belt, he watched her with a vicious glow.

"Want to suck Jack's cock. Where is he? Want to sit on it." With tremendous effort she raised her head and sneered at Dr. Peabody. "Pudding balls! Jack's are rocks. Never felt a dick so hard. Thought he'd rupture me. He HURT but I was FUCKED. FUCKED bloody! FUCKED blind!"

It took an age for Georgie to balance herself in a squat. Her hands were clubs drawing up her nightgown. "I own everything and Cary is not going to marry your son. I shall save her from that ball-less wonder. That ball-less wonder of the western world. Ha! Got to pee!" A harsh contented sound rushed out of Georgie as she leered at Dr. Peabody and urinated on the rug.

"It feels good, Sammy. Better than your cock. Polly owns all your rugs. That's why you're looking so sore. You can't piss on the Persians." Spittle hung from her lower lip and she grinned as Dr. Peabody took three strides and dug his fingers into her hair. He jerked her head back and removed one of his shoes. As she collapsed on her face, he threw his legs over her back.

Georgie could have been animated from a far distance by some faulty control system for the time it took her hands to crawl up past her shoulders and to push until her arms held up her chest and head. Struggling to get up, she didn't realize that she was beneath the bridge of Dr. Peabody's hard legs. As he cracked down on her spine, she groaned with surprise and pleasure.

"Fuck me." She hissed as he jerked back her head. "Fuck!" she exalted. "Like a horse, Sammy. Do it! Do it!"

She screamed as Dr. Peabody brought the thick heel of his loafer down on her head. "Oh, no! Please, no! You're hurting me!" As Georgie shrieked, Dr. Peabody methodically beat her head.

"Tom! Dad! Help mother!" The stair door crashed against the wall as Bailey jumped out into the hall. "Help mother!"

Dr. Peabody completely ignored Bailey as she punched his back. As his arms carried up the loafer and smashed it down on Georgie's head, Bailey could have been pushing at a boulder. Screaming for her father and Tom, she ran into Tom's room.

The rifle was standing in the corner against his dresser. Bailey knelt and clicked off the safety before she picked it up. Its heaviness was impossible as she lurched into the hall.

Georgie's face was turned on the rug. One of her hands had found her head, the other stalled by her ear. Her pale eyes looked steadily at her as the thick heel came down.

"Bailey!" she shrieked.

Yelling for her father, Bailey pointed the rifle at Dr. Peabody. Turning slowly, he took her in with easy contempt. Tossing the loafer away, he put his hand on the end of the rifle and pushed it down.

"What have we here?"

A violent blow in the stomach as she pulled the trigger drove Bailey onto her knees. She dropped the rifle and stared at Dr. Peabody from the bottom of a terrifying pain. She couldn't breathe. Swinging off Georgie, swiftly and gently Dr. Peabody pushed Bailey down on her back and pulled up her legs. She looked up into the sarcasm of his serious eyes and felt her breath come into her lungs as he pressed her knees against her chest. Tom was shouting at his father upstairs.

Next to her, on his knees, Dr. Peabody undid his belt and slipped own his slacks.

"Excuse me, Bailey. Let me just take a look. Feels hot, not much pain, wonder if I can walk." Zipping up, he glanced at Bailey with his usual stern indifference. "I believe you've shot me in the ass." He looked round at Georgie and gave an icy laugh. "She's lying in her own filth and I've got a bullet in my you-know-where."

He was still but for the movement of his eyes. "Why did she call you, Bailey? Your father's upstairs. So is Tom." He watched her with calm curiosity. "Georgie picked the littlest one in her hour of need." Using his arms and one knee, he hitched over to Georgie and gently felt her head.

"I'm sure it looked absolutely brutal, but I was really play-acting. I was in complete control of myself. I'm feeling a few small bumps. You mustn't worry, Bailey. Your mother's passed out from liquor. Get your father down here." He was suddenly frantic. "He's got to call an ambulance."

Cary leaned over the banister as Bailey climbed the stairs. "That shot?" She whispered. She pushed her stunned face close to Bailey's and tried to decipher the little squeaks that struggled from her chest.

Tom was sitting just where she'd left him, with his face on his knees. Her father had changed into his pajamas and bathrobe and was reading in his chair. Her faint yelps finally roused him from his book but his polite attention was so distant that Bailey, breathless and weeping, tugged at him and punched his shoulder in her effort to get him out of his chair.

On his knees, leaning to one side, Dr. Peabody was still feeling Georgie's head. He directed Cary through the bedroom door. He looked urgently at Bailey, understood that her father was just behind her and kept on directing

Cary. Georgie would need slacks and a warm sweater. Forget shoes. Thick woolen socks were enough for her feet.

"Where is he?" he glared at Bailey, his voice a snarl of fear.

Bailey dashed back up the stairs and almost knocked her father down. Tugging him, she felt his hand shake in hers. As he stepped out into the hall, the strong light seemed to wither and bend him.

Dr. Peabody sat on his haunches, his back as straight as a line. He glanced at the rifle, met Jack Bailey's eyes, and then gazed with martial pride at the molding of the hall door.

"I expect you want to kill me, Jack. But, first, you must call an ambulance. Snap out of it," he barked. "Get to the phone"

As his bewildered eyes took in Georgie, lying in the nightgown with her bottom higher than her head, and Dr. Peabody, commanding his stricken body like a proud horseman – one leg of his slacks was black with blood – Jack Bailey's body looked more and more like a dead tree, hollow and shaking in the wind.

"I'll call Memorial?"

"Not on your life. This would be all over town. Georgie and I are going to City Emergency." Dr. Peabody had been holding his thigh, and now terrified Jack Bailey by the blood on his fingers.

"I've heard the doctors don't speak English there," he said in the incongruous tone of polite conversation.

"No one speaks English there," Dr. Peabody wryly

informed him. "But the surgeon is competent, Jack, and luckily for us, he can't tell one white man from another."

Cary came in from the bedroom with a mincing step. She placed the clothes carefully beside Georgie, then stood and plucked up the hem of her bathrobe. When Bailey stooped and flattened Georgie's legs to the rug, Cary sucked in her cheeks and shrank back. Dr. Peabody watched Bailey's struggle to dress her mother and said with caustic approval, "there's the littlest one again and doing very well."

Jack Bailey came to the bedroom door. He encouraged Dr. Peabody with a whiff of a gesture and his faint voice shook as he announced the promised speed of the ambulance's arrival.

"I think it would be wise if I pretended to be you tonight, Jack."

Jack Bailey quickly agreed, and as Cary handed Bailey a sock, she also agreed that a family quarrel would best describe the situation that the ambulance drivers would find.

"If you'll just go upstairs, Jack, I'll say that Georgie and I had too much to drink and got into a nasty fight. I hit her and she ran to get the rifle. She only meant to scare me with it, but when I tried to take it from her, the thing went off. Husband and wife, a bullet in the ass, a hundred bucks for the ambulance crew – they won't report it to the police. They'll be too rich and too amused."

Bailey stepped close to Dr. Peabody and clutched his arms. Her knees shook so hard she could barely stand.

"I shot you! It was me!"

"Nonsense." She was nowhere in his efficient, serious gaze. "I'm looking at a badly frightened child, Jack. You must take care of her."

Tom had not come down to the hall. He hadn't seen a thing. Bailey slipped past her father and was on the third floor landing before he'd climbed five steps. Tom's mind did not have a picture of the drastic occurrence, and Bailey raced to plant herself in front of him and find absolution in the blankness of his brain – for she could not live!

He was still sitting on the floor by the door with his arms wrapped round his drawn-up legs. His forehead was still on his knees.

"Tom" She pressed his sneaker with her foot. "I shot Dr. Peabody. Please, Tom. Tell me what to do."

He looked up at her for a second with desperately squeamish eyes. Bailey felt she was standing at the mouth of a cave and freezing in the cold of its hostile interior. Her father finally came through the door and stood in front of the bookcase with his hands on his hips.

"There's the ambulance, Dad." Bailey went to the window. A red light swept the tops of the trees in a circle as the ambulance stopped before the house. Every few seconds the head of the maple tree appeared in the back sky like a sinister x-ray. Fifty times Bailey saw it before the front door was slammed shut and the ambulance moved up the drive. The siren began at the club gates. Incredible, mocking, deeply serious, it stayed in Bailey's mind forever – the sound of Dr. Peabody's eyes.

Cary came in.

"'But that was in another country,'" Jack Bailey read

126

in a hollow voice. "'Besides, the wench is dead.' I always thought that was Shylock's speech, but here's the play," he flipped the pages, "and it doesn't seem to be here. That's odd don't you think?" As he spoke to her, Cary slowly picked up Georgie's bathrobe and let it drop.

"That's Christopher Marlowe, Dad." Bailey stepped away from the window. He looked anxiously at Cary. "What's the matter? You told me that the first night you were home. Don't you remember?"

"Go down and make coffee, Bailey." Cary wouldn't look at her either. Tom was a morbid cave.

In the kitchen, as she made the coffee, Bailey unknowingly sucked in her cheeks and bowed her shoulders. Tiny steps whisked her here and there and she felt thin as a pencil. The kitchen seemed a vast distance from the rest of the house and she squeaked helplessly while she measured out the coffee and lit the flame beneath the kettle.

Dragging a chair from the table, she stood before the stove, clutching its back. She could not live. The dust in her nose from the china cupboard, the bread box on the table, the toaster and the bottles of spices lined up in twos and marching down the counter all condemned her. How could she live? The stove stood against the yellow wall. The pots hung down – the shape of everything packing her with disgrace.

She turned off the stove and ran out of the kitchen. She ran around the dining room table then walked. With an imploring hand she touched the back of each chair and traced the curves of the table. Last year on her birthday, she was nestled in the curve of the sideboard, just as she was now, and this terrible feeling was still so far away. She could live back then. There she was not disgraced.

Help me! Help me! Help me! she silently pleaded, with every beat of her heart.

Chapter 17

"I shot Dr. Peabody! Tom! Cary! What am I going to do?" Bailey clutched her arm, pulled at her braids and jersey while she entreated the averted faces of her family. They were so squeamish! Bouncing before them, staring into their faces, they had dog's eyes, sliding away. Dr. Peabody wasn't angry at her, they said. Nothing was going to happen to her. Go to sleep, they told her. In the morning, when she woke up, it would all seem like a bad dream. There was nothing to be afraid of – nothing whatever.

Bailey raced away more frightened than before. She did not want to live her life as though she were dreaming, and the third floor, intolerable five minutes ago, became the goal of her frantic climb through the house. She burst in on her father. Holding his book between himself and her persecution, he shrank back in his chair.

"Go to sleep," he begged her. "In the morning you'll see that nothing is going to happen to you. It will feel like a nightmare – nothing more. Go down to your bed, now. Please, please, go to sleep!"

Her father's fear of her pressed a picture of the cellar into her mind and she fled downstairs to the one room she hadn't visited. The huge, white furnace, the washing machine would absolve her.

Oh, that poor Asian soldier that she'd seen on the evening news! He was running under the flames that his uniform and skin were fueling. She'd thought his pain was obscene. She'd hated him! Good, good! Now she was paid back. The furnace, the washing machine, the narrow, dirty windows set high in the stone wall thought her pain was disgusting and they hated her. Good! She deserved it!

Many a time, Bailey had felt herself loathsome. But before, when she was holed up with her disgrace, there had been waves to ride, a raveling down to rest before the next round. This was so steady! Aghast, Bailey wept on the stairs. The most hated girl in school had once been looking out the window during math. She wants to be that tree, Bailey had thought. Susan Gregg wishes she were inanimate.

By the kitchen clock it was six in the morning and Bailey went outside. Her breath was visible as she loped up the drive, clutching her arms in the cold. The tall clubhouse chimneys were a few shades lighter than the gray, winter sky. Her birthday morning, the day that she'd turned ten, had poured between the handsome chimneys and made her a present of a blue block of sky. Her favorite bird had been lavish with its song, its mellow, incredulous cry greeting her repeatedly as she'd walked up the drive.

"It's your birthday, isn't it? Well, what do you think of that?"

In despair Bailey stared at the space between the chimneys. In another few years, wouldn't she remember that radiant block of sky just the way she'd remembered the tunnel of flying yellow tiles? There was no fairyland.

No other worlds. High up on the hill, above the club, there was always the dam. Bailey stopped and listened to the long slide of the water.

"Things happen," she softly said, "one way."

She turned and ran back to the house. She sped to fill her family's minds with the grit and noise of what had happened. Flying, she must stop their magical memories from turning her blood and bones, her mass and misery, into colored air.

Tom didn't go to school that day. He stayed behind the locked door of his room and blocked out Bailey with his stereo. Her head wrapped in her red bandanna, Cary spent the morning vacuuming the house. The loud whine of the motor kept Bailey's voice from reaching her ears and whenever she saw the child she would suck in her cheeks and push the machine with frigid concentration.

Jack Bailey wore gray flannels and Bailey's favorite tweed jacket. He was robust and reassuring. Georgie had woken this morning fit as a fiddle and as soon as Dr. Peabody was fitted with a pair of crutches and had signed out, he'd be bringing her home in a taxi.

"'Tell Bailey it's only a flesh wound and send her my best'. That's what he said, my dear. When I told him you were worrying, he urged me to think of a treat that would buck you up. You'll need to neaten up a little – brush your hair, get a clean jersey – we're going to Bailey Street. I asked Mother if she still had those photos of you and she said that she looks at them every day when she polishes the glass. Get a move on, honey! Your Grandma's cooking steak for lunch with French fries."

When she'd fallen off her bike on the gravel drive and scraped a patch of skin from her thigh, the pain had taken her breath away and she'd run into the woods. Now, before her father, she felt her soul was scraped.

"I can't go there, now." She turned and ran out of the room.

It had begun to rain again and she saw herself running on the golf course, running all afternoon in the cold rain, but her legs gave out at the end of the driveway and she crept to the chestnut tree and hauled herself up on a thick, low branch.

Susan Gregg read worse than she did and was famously ugly. She was always looking out the window, always wishing she could turn into a tree.

As Bailey lay along the branch, its cold, unfeeling bulk passionately engaged her imagination. What would it be like not to feel? Staring at the black bark an inch from her eyes, shivering in the icy drizzle, Bailey struggled to know.

"Oh God!" Georgie cried as Bailey jumped out of the chestnut tree. "What are you doing? Let him get out of the rain, will you?" Georgie's voice was a needle of irritation. "Tell her to move, Sam. Let go of him, Bailey. What the hell's the matter with you?"

"Tell the police," Bailey shrieked on the verge of hysteria, "Tell them I shot you!"

"The police?" Georgie sneered. "Do you want to go to reform school?"

"Yes!"

"Oh, Christ! Don't we need that? A kid in reform school? It was ludicrous to shoot him, Bailey. Plain ludicrous, but not so very serious. Oh, stop crying!" She pushed Bailey off the walk. "Won't you? Won't you?"

"Do you mind, Georgie?" Dr. Peabody watched Bailey intently. "This child is badly frightened."

Ringing the bell, Georgie rapped the door with the knocker at the same time. "I'm cold!" she bawled at Cary. When Dr. Peabody passed Bailey into the house, Georgie was slowly climbing the stairs.

"Reform school?" she accused. "What? Jesus H. Christ!"

Bailey shook violently in the warmth of the house. Dr. Peabody took the blanket from the hall couch and wrapped her up. He pushed her gently into the library, closed the door and sat her on the striped couch. Sitting down beside her, he put his hand on her forehead; she admired the creases of his gray pants. Before he'd gone to Stockbridge, the creases of her father's pants had been just as sharp. They rode before his fast legs like ships' prows. Now, his trousers flapped flat against his shins.

"Even if I did have a thermometer, you'd bite it off. Are you getting some warmth from that blanket?"

When he sat back and crossed his legs, she leaned forward. Humor glinted in his pale, cold eyes, like sun on ice, and then, not sympathy, not affection, but the serious interest of his expression kept her eyes glued to his.

"I shouldn't have left you last night. It was unavoidable but too bad, nevertheless. You're suffering from shock, Bailey, and it will pass. It doesn't matter that you know you're innocent – you are, you know." He briefly gripped her shoulder. "You must still react to what happened."

133

"I shot you." Bailey gasped.

"What happened was violent and terrifying. I got drunk and beat up your mother like a common thug. I should have been killed." His eyes glowed with cold disgust. "But by your father, not you. I haven't blushed in a dog's age and I can't bring myself to imagine what you must be feeling. God!" He shuddered with revulsion. "A ten-year-old girl shouldn't have to take the place of her father. You've been imposed on! Horribly imposed on!"

"Call the police, please!"

"You don't understand that you're suffering from shock. I do, and I tell you it will pass."

"It won't," Bailey whispered. "I can't live here anymore. I want to go to jail."

"Did you ever see the Wooster Reformatory?" he gently teased.

Bailey eagerly remembered the perfectly square, perfectly bare red brick building before Dr. Peabody could characterize it as that ghastly box with rows of tiny barred windows. It was set in the middle of a vast lawn, as bare as the building except for a long loop of drive and the two huge pine trees that stood like green-skirted giants at the narrow door.

"It's filled with black girls, Bailey. They'd have a field day with you."

"Only at first." Bailey relished the bullying. "Blacks in jail are just as dumb as me. I could go back to the beginning there and learn it all again. I could learn a trade." She pointed to the TV. "I saw a program about it. Girls learn to fix cars. They have sports."

Dr. Peabody stood up with an apprehensive smile. "Snap out of this, damn it. You're going to feel much better in a day or two."

Staring at the sharp creases that ran down his long, muscular legs, Bailey saw her father's frail shins, his wrinkled legs, and felt a ton of misery drop her to the rug.

"I want to go there! You don't understand! I've got to be reformed!"

She felt a light hand on her head, heard his cautious step and the turning of the door handle.

"Give yourself another day, my dear. You'll feel normal again. I promise you."

Couldn't eat, couldn't sleep, Bailey roamed the house that night. Oddly enough, it was in the upstairs hall where she'd shot Dr. Peabody that she could pause the longest before the push of shame and disgrace moved her on. She'd sit cross-legged on the gold-colored rug and stare down at the faint bloodstain that Cary couldn't wash away. The stone house had stood against a strong wind that day. Some gusts were violent.

At the reform school, the giant evergreens would sway and creak with powerful solemnity. The tiny barred windows looked out on the silent sermon and agreed that the bleak sky, the rough, icy wind were nature's gift to the criminal girls. It darkened and chilled the sullen walls and reform went quicker.

The rain kept on into Saturday and Bailey went in and out of the rooms in double-time. The whole family was at home and uneasy in her company. The Peabodys were invited to dinner and Georgie, driven almost mad by Bailey's sighs and nervous hands, ordered Cary to let her help cook. Dropping eggs on the floor, scattering the flour, Bailey couldn't break through Cary's silent distress. She climbed the stairs to the third floor but the sound of her father reading whipped her around. She could feel his voice, as though punched from an empty barrel; she could feel it in her own chest.

When Tom went out briefly, Bailey slipped into his room and shut the door. He said nothing about the wreckage he found on his return. Turning from his desk as he came in, Bailey passionately apologized about his ruined typewriter even while her hands were twisting the keys.

"It's okay," he mumbled while she tried to look into his hostile, frightened eyes. "Don't worry about it. I've got to take a shower. Talk to you later."

It was strange that Dr. Peabody's great seriousness could not be called concern and yet, she had no other word for his direct, efficient look. He put his drink on her bedside table and stood up. Frowning at the blue glider which slowly turned, he read out her name as a troublesome question and touched the wings with his careful, light fingers.

"Does it fly?"

"Dad made it for me. It flies like a dream."

"You will too" he snapped. "I don't believe in giving children pills. I was certain you'd sleep last night and yet, you say you didn't." His sharp distrust soothed her. "I'll go down and get the red ones. Wouldn't put a fly down. Buzz, buzz, yourself." Bailey had never received his smile before and flushed with pleasure.

"I mean that one of those pills can't harm you."

"A swallow won't hurt me either," she murmured to herself. When she heard him on the stairs she reached for his drink. Except for the surprising taste – the clear, calm liquid looked wildly delicious – it was like drinking the sun. By the third swallow, Bailey tipped back her head and drank off the glass as quickly as she could.

She ran to the bathroom, filled the glass with water and barely managed to wet the rug beside the bed before Dr. Peabody came back into the room. Apologizing for knocking over his drink, she crawled under the covers and held out her hand for the pill.

What a fuss people made over liquor. She didn't feel it at all. Her hands were still for the first time all day. She lay quietly against her pillow and when Dr. Peabody came from the bathroom with a full water glass she thought he was the handsomest man she'd ever seen.

"Good night, Bailey."

He took back the glass and stroked her bangs to the side. "You're going to sleep like a baby. I want you to wake up like a baby – feeling that you're innocent. You see that I'm not using those damn crutches. I don't need them. There's a tiny hole in my leg and in a few days I won't be limping."

Her blood was going through her body so strongly that the bed felt alive and traveling in soft circles.

"There are no pictures of me. I've looked and looked." His amusement was exciting. "My grandmother has me under glass on her dressing table. Bailey Street!" she belted it out and fell back against the pillow. "You drive through a long tunnel to get there. I used to go all the time, but now I can't."

A handsome god stood at the end of her bed. As he said her mother's name, Bailey saw a beautiful woman with a soft and friendly face. She was in the blue Mercury Convertible, her mother and father in the front seat and herself sitting between them. Yellow tiles were flying by, and cigarette smoke streamed from their mouths, smelling delicious.

They were both so gay and they thrilled her with their compliments. Her father tugged up the visor of her baseball cap to smile at her.

"You're terrific!" He said.

"And smart," said Georgie, "and good!"

Her father laughed. "Good as gold. Look at that sun. It was winter when we started through the mountain and now it's spring." Lifting her cap, Bailey smiled from one to the other.

"It's a miracle, folks!" Georgie hugged her. "She's adorable! The pick of the litter. My girl Bailey."

Chapter 18

Sitting at the dinner table, Mrs. Hughes covered her ears at Bailey's friendly greeting to the waitress and directed a spiteful glance at Jim Peabody's discarded friend.

"She's un-teachable – unforgivably stubborn." Jim brushed the lapels of his blue blazer.

"A most timely discovery with your father arriving for the Sunday banquet." Enjoying her own malice, Mrs. Hughes kept careful track of the boy's response. Her ridiculing of the girl could sometimes provoke a strange anger, a moody retreat, which, never lasting any length of time, could nonetheless jeopardize the luncheon that tomorrow she would share with Jim Peabody and his celebrated father.

Samuel Peabody was a recent widower and a man should enjoy the rejuvenation afforded to him by a handsome woman. The thought of the past year's curbing of her girth, her thighs in particular, gave a lustful flare to her anticipation.

"It is the stupidest thing for Bailey to jog the hour before dinner."

"Well, darling, if she must go running twice a day."

"There's no excuse for excess." Jim tossed the menu onto the empty plate beside him and held his head. "My program for Bailey was sensible, moderate and balanced. Two hours of running a day?" Jim fumed.

"To come panting into the dining room?"

"Beet-red, sweating, shouting – so ugly."

"This morning she ran into town." Jim sneered at the remembered sight from Mrs. Hughes's car. "That brittle macadam surface in sneakers? If she hasn't rooked her feet already – she will."

"Finally, she's taking off that hideous wool cap. Wonder of the world! Why, Jim, she must have been jogging to Stockbridge's own beauty palace because her hair is simply chopped off."

Twisting round, Jim took sharp measure of the jaunty-looking girl before his resentment could interfere.

"One should never trust the locals with hair. How pathetic, Jim. Bailey looks like the boys packing boxes in the supermarket or at the station pumping gas. Don't you think so?"

"She looks suitable."

"Oh, ho! Now that you've dropped her she can be as ugly as she chooses?"

"No!" Jim rapped out then blushed in confusion.

It was his day-to-day impression of Bailey during the two weeks since she'd invalidated their friendship by talking as he hated her to talk, that she was rushing from the blind past where she'd adored him, that her swiftly emerging memories were the fuel of her vitality and that her eyes expressed a regretful impatience with his wounded pride.

He saw that sympathy had replaced the worship in her

eyes and that she was lonely. Jim turned again to look at her, rebuking her presumption of equality.

"Her manners are annoying, I agree." Mrs. Hughes tapped his wrist. "But she'll never interpret criticism from your gaze alone. And really, Jim, you can't want her over here."

"I don't," he whispered, cold as Iceland.

"The Salisbury steak requires energy but it's tasty." Her teeth clicking on her fork, Mrs. Hughes gave a nod of encouragement. "Eat and be thankful that you've emerged from the insanity of introducing that bizarre soul to your father."

"She would have been uncomfortable."

"Uncomfortable?"

"See it straight, Jim. That girl would find a lunch with your father the most horrible experience of her young life. I'm pleased you won't have that on your conscience."

Whenever Mrs. Hughes verified the character of the cruel, censoring doctor, Jim's pride was momentarily soothed and he could forgive himself for misrepresenting his emasculation as a physical castration. Mrs. Hughes was right on target – that no experience in Bailey's past could possibly prepare her for the brutal exposure of every stupidity, weakness and confusion that came under his father's keen notice. A sarcasm sharp as a scalpel had unmanned his son as surely as an operation.

If he'd spoken in metaphor, he hadn't lied; Jim wanted to shout after Bailey as she left the dining room. How could a young boy deal with the violent dislike which had always seemed to flow from his father's eyes into his very blood?

Even his mother had pitied his youthful helplessness but, ridiculed herself, could only offer the future as hope – her constant consolation so nervously whispered of his "wonderful life after Daddy's death."

At bridge after dinner, Jim was so deeply involved in moral justification with Bailey that he ruined three rubbers for Mrs. Hughes and for the first time he saw relief in her eyes when he got up from the card table to go to his room.

"Imagine your nerves at your father's visit if you'd had that ghastly girl to introduce. Take a sedative tonight, Jim. I don't like that look in your eye."

Jim stopped in front of Bailey's room while he slipped his key from his pocket. She'd made a Christmas star and taped it to her door. Inside, she was singing along to a commercial carol and doing what? Reading? Watching the glider turning in her model house? Jim thought of the glider turning in the tiny dark room and, as though his imagination were in competition with the girl's porous mind, he suddenly saw rows of eyeglass frames on plastic shelves against a white wall.

Plunging into his room, he closed the door and leaned against it. Dreading the scourge of more images, his heart beat hard while he undressed and put on his pajamas to watch the evening news.

Why should one remember what one couldn't change and never intended? Jim watched the television scenes of daily disaster with grim dedication to his life's philosophy.

Unmanly, all his life a bum – that he knew, so what good would it do to dredge up a particular crime, to enter Bailey's past life, to be her blond young man?

He could continue to live a numb life as remote to himself as a doomed antique hero, but he could not accept that each day he'd gone to work, fitted glasses and toyed with Bailey's sister in drunken amnesia. He could not!

Brushing his teeth, Jim spied on his face in the mirror. The look Mrs. Hughes hadn't liked was the look of a coward. Two sleeping pills in his mouth, Jim got into bed. The image of a pathetic victim began to dissolve in jeering detail. Shelves of eyeglass frames, and now he saw his feet on a brick sidewalk. Black loafers in sluggish advance — the pills could not work fast enough to save the cowardly victim from detail's devastation — day after day his reluctant feet taking him to work.

The year Bailey had been ten, he'd never been lower. The thrust of the exiting subway passengers delivered him to Marlborough Street where the brick sidewalk was a guiding code to his dead feet. Right, left, right, left, to dismal occupation. All day he was slipping glasses on and off faces, and at the bars every night he flooded the day's memories, to wake the next morning with a blank brain.

Hearing Bailey in her room as the night went by, he wanted to cry out or knock on the wall for her help, but the sleeping pills had pegged down his body. His stony body and his guilty mind seemed permanent punishment and then he woke up in the light of dawn. Standing at his window, he watched the motion of the earth — the misty woods parting from the sun — the motion that was bringing his father to the sanitarium's front door.

Chapter 19

"Her name is Bailey," Jim answered his father, but too softly for Dr. Peabody to hear him.

"Come again?"

"Bailey?" Jim whispered.

"I'll be damned if I know. I'm asking you."

Pitying Jim who looked at her in pale appeal, Mrs. Hughes could hardly muster her own voice as the celebrated surgeon turned his head to her. Tall, weathered, with shorn white hair and icy bright eyes, the smile of his thin lips seemed a mockery of cordiality. From the moment he'd uncrossed his lean, long legs and stood at the luncheon table to greet his son's guest, Mrs. Hughes abandoned the excitement of physical appeal – she'd dressed with girlish thrill – and ordered her mind to stand steadfast before the chill of his measuring look.

Shaking hands, she almost curtsied and when she turned to greet Jim, she was startled by the sorrowful debility he suffered at his father's side. His army jacket, now thankfully discarded, had been the costume of a wistful child.

"Our most famous patient," said Mrs. Hughes with ironic emphasis. "At fourteen years old, she's the youngest alcoholic ever to find herself shut up at Stockbridge. I believe she calls herself Bailey."

"Bailey?" Harshly incredulous, the doctor's gaze insulted Mrs. Hughes as though he suspected her to be of careless mind.

"Did you say her name is Bailey?"

"Her only name – or so she says. She says rather a lot and all of it appalling."

From across the room Bailey turned her head to meet the doctor's gaze. Her bobbed hair in a pretty swirl, she nodded and smiled with casual dignity.

"But do you know her?" Mrs. Hughes was flirtatiously curious.

"I'll say I know her," the doctor wanted to say. "She shot me in the ass when she was ten years old."

What he would have said if Mrs. Hughes had been a friend and a person of compassion, was that Bailey was the daughter of his mistress and one evening, four years ago, had fired at him with a hunting rifle to protect her mother from his drunken blows.

Her family had shunned her after the shooting and allowed her to shut herself up in her bedroom while she drank vodka and watched family shows on television. Bailey was sober in the morning, for her sleeps were long and deep and she always went to school. But she learned nothing. The principal suggested that Bailey board at a famous academy for the mentally challenged.

Anticipating a renewal of her memory when Bailey stopped drinking and eager to discount her memories as illusions, Dr. Peabody urged her parents to send her to Stockbridge, a mental hospital on the western border of the state.

He would keep track of Bailey's rehabilitation and pay the bills.

He was true to both promises, but he could not face her. Bailey had been delivered to Stockbridge as if she were a large package. Georgie Bailey handed her over to the receptionist and drove away. None of her family visited, as though her transformation from a keen-eyed child to a pleasantly smiling hulk with sad, vague eyes was a crime they must deny. Dr. Peabody glanced at his son with carping respect.

"Why, you've only been tutoring Bailey a few months. There's intelligence and focus in her gaze. I didn't recognize her."

With pity for her slighted self, the dowager glanced at Jimmy. Poor, subdued fellow – good grief that she'd even thought him handsome or even bright.

"Your son, sir, is responsible for the girl's improvement. She was a gray cloud before his attention. He's been magnificent. He's changed her life."

"We're friends," Jim said with a woeful pull of his mouth. "We read together and walk."

"You taught the girl to read?"

"It's repetition, Dad. Over and over. Bailey never minded."

"Didn't you?"

"When Bailey gets it, she keeps it." Jim smiled with a tense mouth. "It's been great fun."

"Oh, poo! Fun for a while, I should say." Mrs. Hughes spoke loudly to draw the doctor's attention. "Your son hit a brick wall when he tried to change the girl's accent."

"Go ask her to join us, Jim. I should like us to meet."

Nodding inane apology at Mrs. Hughes, Jim jumped to his feet. Following the girl back to the table, her cordial acceptance bright as her yellow sweater, his smile dropped dead at the sight of the dowager's vindictive eyes.

Bailey saluted the distinguished doctor as he got to his feet.

"I'm crazy about your creases – in your trousers," she laughed. "You could be military. In fact, sir, you remind me of my father before he went away to war."

"Which war, my dear?" Dr. Peabody took a chair from the next table and bade Bailey sit beside him. Hailing the waitress, he requested another place set for his guest.

"Oh," Bailey twirled her hands, "just the war. My father said my mother was one war behind and I cannot repeat what she said back to him – at least not here."

"Can't I imagine," said the surgeon.

"Really? So you know her? Do you know my mother?"

"I should say I know her type. As you can see, my dear, I'm old enough to know all the types."

"So, do you?"

"I gather not."

"He'd rather not, he means. Oh, don't be disgusted, Jim." Bailey winked into the surgeon's frosty face. "Your son thinks I'm a dreadful social climber. But I think I met him long ago. When I was ten, I made Jim a hero."

Dr. Peabody glanced wryly at his distressed son. "A hero?"

Could the doctor stand to hear one more thing? The creases in his trousers gave her the same thrill of mysterious familiarity. His long legs were so crisp and mean.

Jim watched the waitress and the gestures of Mrs. Hughes's angry dejection as she sat ignored on the doctor's left.

"I must compliment my dry-cleaner. I'm sure he doesn't appreciate his power to excite such eloquent emotion. But you are really quite fascinating. What other mysterious memories do you have?"

"I'm not fascinating," Bailey blushed with delight. "But Cary and Tom are – and Mother! Beautiful Mother, my father adored her and oh, my darling stone house and the pine trees and the gigantic club swimming pool with salt water piped in from the bay – I helped to clean it in the spring and fall – and the two stone lions that guarded the clubhouse steps! Tom and I went on the longest rides before he got so dumb. My father kept everything in perfect repair – perfect – and he would never allow any gentlemen inside the clubhouse without a jacket and a tie and even my mother couldn't wear trousers except in the privacy of her own home."

"It seems a fairly satisfactory memory."

"My mother is so beautiful! She's so smart and so funny like a comedian on television – Tom and I roll on the floor laughing at her. She's perfect." Bailey paused in sudden worry. "Except she forgets everything."

"It's true you don't have a personal name?"

"She forgot to name me." Bailey's eyes went dull with dread. Her father died before I was born, she nearly died herself with grief, and she couldn't remember the name she had picked for me. Poor mother!"

"Nonsense."

Jim marveled at his father's blunt equality, as though Bailey were an erring colleague. "Your mother was drunk the night you were born. I was there."

Squinting with hatred, Bailey thrust out her chin.

"In a pig's eye. You son of a bitch!"

The ensuing silence of the small, crowded dining room rang in Jim's ears as loudly as Bailey's furious outburst. Looking at his plate, he counted the seconds of freakish quiet to five when a trill of mocking laughter draped privacy around the table and Jim dared to glance up at his father.

His chair pushed back from the table, one leg crossed over his knee, the celebrated surgeon looked at Bailey with amused forbearance.

"I was tactless."

"My mother is beautiful! Bailey's gaze held the doctor's in stubborn demand.

"Indeed, she is."

"Indeed, Captain Peabody, thanks to your son, who's the world's best teacher, one day I'm going to write a story about my family."

"A fairy story, no doubt." Raising his water glass, Dr. Peabody toasted the girl. "Here's to Mama, so lovely and loving and kind."

"My mother hated you, Dr. Creases, Lord of the Manor. Didn't we hear her? At the top of the house, over the kettle drums." Slack in her chair, her eyes heavy with indolent lust, Bailey crooned in her new accent, the accent of her mother, the accent of Jim's harsh demand.

"Kettle me, Sammy, God, I'm kettle. I need a good kettle. I want to kettle, kettle, kettle. Do it, Captain, handsome Sammy, Polly's baby boy. Hell's bells! Jack knows how but he's not here. Gotta pee, Sammy. The rug feels good, baby boy, better than your cock. Polly owns all the rugs in your house. Isn't that why you're looking so sore? Isn't it, Sammy? You can't get drunk and piss on Polly's persians."

For the first time since the beginning of dinner, Dr. Peabody looked at his other guest, as Mrs. Hughes, in crimson embarrassment and rasping stockings, hurried from the dining room.

"Poor lady," Bailey murmured in a sickened voice. "God, Jimmy, I could never talk like that, don't you see?"

"I'm glad," the young man whispered.

"Speak up!" commanded Dr. Peabody with a vicious thrust of his chin.

"Long ago, in a stone house," the girl boomed in Jim's silence, "lived a little girl and her name was Bailey. Her family was everything to her, but one day, seeing a beautiful blond prince run by – he was fleeing his murderous dad – she followed him like a starving dog and never went home again."

"Fairy tales," the doctor scoffed with unsettled eyes.

"That's what I see, ole daddy long legs. Look, Jim! I see one now." Tapping his arm she pointed to the nearby window where, in red mittens and the captain's jacket Dr. Peabody had worn with distinction in the last war, Stockbridge's gardener marched by, a snow shovel on his shoulder.

"How pompous," Bailey laughed.

"Absurdly pompous, my dear." Dr. Peabody turned his angry contempt from the gardener to his son. "But happily for the man he is ignorant of his state."

As the gardener grew small in the window, Jim Peabody could imagine his father's influence in his own mind retreating to a blessed speck. One day, might he not be as free as this girl? His heart boiled with hope.

"Tell me, my dear. Did the prince and the little girl ever get out of the forest?"

"On schedule," Jim spoke out.

Getting up, Bailey thanked the famous doctor for lunch and turned her smile on his withered son. "See you at four, Jimmy."

Chapter 20

"If you promise not to make a fuss about church next Sunday, I'll let you drive." Georgie and Tom stood side by side before the hall mirror, both brushing their hair.

"Moods are like the weather, don't you think, except that with moods there's no forecasting. Today my heart is the sun, my lungs, the dry and radiant sky. Corpuscles play in my sparkling red rivers and my organs bask." Putting down the brush, Georgie nudged Tom with her elbow. "I've never seen you with a more attractive haircut. Your tweed jacket and navy blue shirt – could you possibly be more handsome?"

Tom dragged on his cigarette and cleared his bangs from his eyes with a toss of his head, "It's the Georgie A-1," he croaked at Bailey.

"It ain't government-inspected," Bailey called from the stairs.

"But, it's choice, man. Top quality. The BEST!"

"What?" Georgie laughed.

"Your mood!" the children cried.

"Mood," Georgie mused before her image in the mirror. She wore a gray tweed suit. Bailey had polished her black pumps and her silk shirt was just back from the cleaners. Brushing her shoulders, her particular smell –

leather and cold sky – came back to Bailey, as she admired her thoroughbred legs.

"Mood is a convergence of factors, chemical, environmental. Hey Bailey, did you hear about the lady in New York City who planted some marijuana seeds in the courtyard of her apartment building? When she woke up the next morning there was this eerie green light in her bedroom."

Tom took the car keys from the pantry shelf and closed the kitchen door behind them. As he backed the car from the garage, Georgie put her arm around Bailey's shoulders and gently tugged her braid as she talked.

"The woman crept to the window and my God, if there wasn't an enormous pot plant shooting a mile up in the sky."

"That's Jack and the Beanstalk." Bailey glowed from stem to stern as Georgie kissed the top of her head.

"I've never seen such a quiet light," said her mother. "On a day like this it's easy to sense, but do you ever doubt that there is a fairyland?"

"Never!" Tom pointed to the church where Georgie made them go every Sunday. According to Tom, the priest had them all down on their knees worshipping a carbon atom. Georgie shrugged off Tom's theories about the origin of life. They had nothing to do with her promise to their father that while he was off and fighting in this dreadful war, his family would go to church and pray for him. She'd sworn on the Bible. Bah! Just another congregation of molecules, to Tom's scientific mind.

"Quarks, the structure of our minds, Bailey's spiffy blue jacket. I don't care what form of fairyland I worship."

Reaching across her daughter, Georgie patted Tom's knee. "Physics to you, I know. Listen to what I read yesterday – you're driving very well – I tried to memorize it. I think – yes. Is it possible that all the different particles might be the different state of motion of some underlying structure of substance? Very possible. There's always something underlying. Take those huge metal things." Georgie pointed to the tract of land beside the highway where towers relayed electricity from the city where they were headed into the countryside.

"Those towers were constructed by men from small pieces of steel. They weren't intended to look like Puritan ministers. But don't they?"

Both Bailey and Tom suddenly saw the menaced woods and fields.

"If I looked up at that same tower in Italy or Africa – if the tower were removed from all the associations of this locale, would I still see the iron men, the stern patricians looming with disapproval?"

"You see with the mind, Mother." Tom tossed his cigarette into the wind. "Seeing is interpretation."

"Then fuck the mind. But not today. Today the mind is friendly."

In the heart of the city, Bailey got out of the car then looked back at her mother as she drove off to find a parking space. Georgie was driving toward the river and her mood was an unbelievable, double A-1.

Tom let the heavy glass door fall back on Bailey and with a toss of his head, stepped up to the receptionist. The girl was reading and didn't look up. Smiling, he leaned on the counter.

"You're staring at me because I'm so handsome. The name's Tom Bailey," he informed the blank face. "We've only got twenty minutes."

Looking at her long, crimson nails, the receptionist told them to go sit down. Mr. Guster would be going for his lunch when he finished with his customer, and they would have to wait for the new young man. He was always late.

There were four wooden tables in the optician's small shop. Glass shelves carrying rows of frames covered the back and side walls. The sun came brightly through the font window and Bailey could see the city reflected in a hundred details from the lenses all around her.

Across the room, a woman in a tall fur hat was trying on glasses. As Tom passed by her to hang up his jacket, the sleeve brushed the woman's shoulder. He apologized and then stood smiling at the frigid face as though he'd gotten the warmest response in the world. He drew up a spare chair with the tip of his shoes and sat down beside her.

As Mr. Guster straightened the frames on the woman's face, he glanced curiously at Tom. Bailey was amazed at her brother's loud, confident tone as he told the woman that his mother had chosen the very frame she held in her hands and had been very happy with it. The bluish tint looked as well outdoors as it did inside.

"They sit down next to you. They talk to you. They chew gum in your ear." The woman frowned and spoke into a small mirror. "I'm certainly not sold on the color, but I've tried on every frame in the store."

"They look terrific! My mother has a pair." Tom tossed his head with an eager smile.

"Ghastly color." The woman turned her back on Tom and sighed with irritation. "Oh, just charge them up." Standing, she latched her fur coat. "You'll have them for me in a week," she decreed and almost ran over Tom as she talked over her shoulder going to the door. "I'd hoped to see Jim while I was here. I certainly expect to see him this evening."

"Why did you talk to that lady?" Bailey whispered as Tom sat down beside her.

"I thought I handled that pretty well." As Mr. Guster took the frames from the table and put them back on the shelves, Bailey fumed at Tom's chipper wink. It was new. At home he'd stand for ages in front of a mirror and hold open his left eye, while the muscles of his right lid "caught on."

"Wasn't that Mrs. Samuel Peabody?"

At Mr. Guster's curt affirmation, Tom poked Bailey and sent her up the wall with his serious satisfaction. These days she liked and despised Tom in quick alternation. Lifting them, plunging them down, arguments formed in their lives like waves.

"Today's affirmation is tomorrow's style." Tugging her braid, Tom would do his wink. She was just jealous because he'd won the tennis tournament.

His crap tennis was no target for her jealousy.

"Winning tennis," he blithely corrected.

At times Bailey would rediscover the sweetness in

157

his face and wonder at the oily conceit that mostly coated it. He'd lost his virginity with a girl who adored him and had turned into a preppy asshole! The girl's wealth and classy name made Tom look down on the swimming pool business and he'd forgotten Bailey Street existed. After school, Jack Bailey would hit with him at the indoor court for an hour when his girl would drive up in her yellow convertible and bring a thermos of cocoa into the chilly dome.

Every night at the dinner table, Tom would talk to his father about his girlfriend's social connections while Georgie drank herself into a drunken sneer and Cary carted off the roast, the blood and jutting bone a proper but unseen object for her martyred eyes.

When Mr. Guster left the shop, Tom yawned and picked up a magazine. Hating to hear his restlessness, Bailey got up and looked out the window. She felt so heavy and dull. Then, in a flash, she soared. The handsomest boy she'd ever seen was walking slowly up the street. Glorious!

A few feet from the window, he noticed her, smiled and waved. His hair was blond and dramatic and when he turned, his hand going round to his back pocket; the edge of his profile against the blue sky sent shivers of delight down her spine. At his lips, the small bottle ignited in the sun. When he stepped close to the window Bailey saw a merry kindliness streaming from his eyes. Her color eyes! He put the bottle back in his pocket and sauntered into the shop.

"You're late." The receptionist pointed at him. Her crimson nail switched to Bailey. "She's waiting for glasses."

Unlike Tom, his wink hadn't begun as affectation. He beckoned her to a table and swept out a chair. "Just one more minute," he cried, rushing into the back.

Tom flipped the magazine to the end of the couch and stood up. "I bet Mrs. Peabody is fucking mad!" He yawned and stretched.

Bailey turned round in her chair to look at his face.

"I just acted as if she'd spoken to us, as if she were most graciously interested."

"Why do you think she knows you?" The edge of her eye saw the blond young man come out of the back. He studied her for a moment then turned to the shelves.

"Ding a ling, Bailey. You deserve to be dumb. That was Polly Peabody."

The young man glanced at them over his shoulder.

"You're the idiot, Tom! She didn't look at you once. She thought you were just another fresh kid."

Tom jabbed his chest with his thumb. "She knew who I was!"

"'They sit down next to you, they talk to you, they chew gum in your ear.' You weren't chewing gum. That's just the way she handles uppity micks."

"I'm not a —" blood swooped into Tom's cheeks.

Mrs. Peabody's voice was as clear in Bailey's ears as on the recent Saturday at the Country Club, when she'd moved her golf ball and hid under the bridge.

"That woman could see you a hundred times and she wouldn't separate your face from your accent."

"I don't have an accent anymore."

"Do I?" Bailey sweetly asked.

"I'll say!"

"Big man, Tom. You sound just like me."

Coughing tactfully, the blond young man came up to the table. He put six frames in front of Bailey and swung his leg over the stool.

"He's my brother," Bailey explained as Tom flung himself into the chair at the side of the table. Staring at his humorous mouth, Bailey loved the peppermint smell of his breath and its warmth on her face. She loved the feeling of his fingers on her ears and she wished Tom would stop making a fool of himself, so that she could memorize the face of the man she was going to adore forever.

He'd tip his head when the frame was straight on her face, put his fist under his chin and lean back. Talking like a madman, Tom was desperate to impress him but at the moment she was at the center of his attention. His seriousness was passionate and she felt legitimized in its flow, as though — no more than a bird or a baby — could she be any different than she was. The slight shake of his head, his utterly intelligent smile, introduced her to bliss.

"I can too read." She told him as Tom announced her astonishing illiteracy. Was Tom on something? His hands flew as he lectured the blond young man on the astonishing stupidity of the world.

"My sister's been in the hands of idiots. When someone has a reading problem, the first thing you do is check out the eyes, right? She's got eyeballs like smashed eggs. She can't see!"

"I see great, asshole. Shut up!" The young man's quick, respectful smile completely calmed her down.

"Don't you have parents?" he asked Tom.

"They died in a car accident five years ago. Bailey and I and our older sister, Cary, all live with Dr. Peabody. He's an old family friend and Cary's engaged to his son."

"I know the Peabodys quite well." Tom's shame turned his contempt to pity. I've been unaware of a handful of orphans or a wedding."

"I wish they were dead." Tom muttered then really pushed to justify his lie. As the young man heard about the filthy house, the fistfights and the drinking, Bailey watched the calm green eyes for the disgust that would send her flying into the street.

"My father's the manager of the Country Club."

Tom looked anxiously at the young man, who continued, "He's a Catholic. He believes in the infallibility of the Pope. But my mother is a Jessup."

"That's interesting for around here. How did they get together?"

"At the Country Club. Dad ran the restaurant there when he got out of college. It's murder at home now because my father doesn't want Cary to marry Jim Peabody. He's not a nice Catholic boy."

"It's mother who's against the marriage, because Jim Peabody's a drunk."

Horrified, Bailey was on her feet.

"You lie!" Tom casually whacked the side of her head, then stiffened with fear as the young man took hold of his shirt front and pushed him back in his chair.

"She wouldn't lie! She always tells the truth! You looked like you were hitting your dog."

"You don't know her." Ducking humiliation, Tom became a bullet of contempt. "How about some glasses, pal, we haven't got all day. You can't sell me those. They're ugly! Too dark, too big for her face."

Bailey peered into the mirror and pushed the horn-rimmed frames tagainst her nose. "They're good, I think."

"No way! Try on the steel-rimmed ones."

Bailey glared at Tom through the large frames. "I want those."

"When they're on your face, its 'these.' You look like a coloring book. Thick dark lines on a white page. No way, Bailey."

"It's not you who's paying for them!" she shouted, the white page turning red. "I want them and I'm getting them."

Tom yawned and got to his feet. He stood gracefully while he got out his wallet. Bailey's eye prescription fluttered down from his fingers. While the young man bent and picked it up, Tom sauntered to the shop door and went out. Was he going to leave her? Where was Georgie? As Tom walked past the window, the blond young man followed her anxious gaze.

"The glasses should be charged and sent, please." As Bailey gave him the name and address, she looked long and hard at his hair and hands and wondered again at the ease she felt before him, the purity. Shaking his hand, she felt his warmth like the noon sun and she raced after Tom.

There he was! Georgie was holding his arm, gesturing and smiling as they strolled along.

"I got lost," she told Bailey, laughing. "I always do and I grew up in this city. Everything always looks so different to me." She pressed Bailey's shoulder. "I wonder if we ever really see. Your glasses!" Georgie clapped her hands.

"I'd love to be you the first time you put them on and look about. You'll see an entirely new world, and when you pick up a book you'll be able to read. Fairyland is around the corner, my sweet girl, and only a week to wait."

Georgie stopped dead. Her joy in the redeeming was chased off her face by an expression of hilarious horror. Bailey laughed aloud.

"Oh, my god, there's Polly Peabody!"

As Georgie ducked into an alley, Bailey looked up into the face of the lady who'd despised the existence of herself and Tom in the glasses shop. Then so proudly massive, now she was all quivers from Georgie's slight, even the water in her disbelieving eyes.

"Georgie?" Peering down the alley, Polly Peabody hoped for a joke.

"Mother ran because the time's up on the meter. A week ago our car was towed."

Ignoring Bailey, walking away, Mrs. Peabody stepped on the side of her foot and almost fell in sad and clumsy commotion.

Bailey knocked Tom's arm to stop his soft cheer.

"Shut up," she cried, and returned his punch with the best she had. Who could care about such an asshole when fairyland was right around the corner?

THE END

About the Author

Joan Hawkins was born in Cambridge, Massachusetts. She attended Bennington College and New York University. She has lived most of her life in Manhattan, where she practiced psychotherapy. Her debut novel, *Underwater*, was published by GP Putnam in 1974. The book was critically acclaimed, challenging traditional gender roles and exploring controversial issues of the day. A second edition of *Underwater* was published on its fortieth anniversary by Landon Books in 2014.

Bailey is the author's second novel. Joan's third book, *Trespass* (2013), is a fascinating portrait of a moribund, spirited woman living life joyously to the end. *Rematch (2021)*, set in the early eighties, is a prescient take on corporate sexual discrimination. Joan's fifth work, the political drama *Family Money*, was published by 451 Editions in 2022 along with the electronic edition of *Underwater*.

For more, see: www.JoanHawkins.net

Landon Books, New York